fire

color

one

Jenny Valentine

Philomel Books

fire

color

one

Jenny Valentine

Philomel Books

PHILOMEL BOOKS
an imprint of Penguin Random House LLC
375 Hudson Street, New York, NY 10014

Copyright © 2015 by Jenny Valentine.
First American edition published in 2017 by Philomel Books. Published
in Great Britain by HarperCollins Children's Books in 2015. Penguin
supports copyright. Copyright fuels creativity, encourages diverse
voices, promotes free speech, and creates a vibrant culture. Thank you
for buying an authorized edition of this book and for complying with
copyright laws by not reproducing, scanning, or distributing any part
of it in any form without permission. You are supporting writers and
allowing Penguin to continue to publish books for every reader.

Philomel Books is a registered trademark of Penguin Random
House LLC.

Library of Congress Cataloging-in-Publication Data
Names: Valentine, Jenny, author. | Title: Fire color one / Jenny
Valentine. | Description: New York, NY : Philomel Books, [2017] |
Summary: Following her fortune-hunting mother's plan, a teenaged
arsonist meets her wealthy, dying father, the owner of a priceless
art collection, only to discover that the stories she has been told about
him all her life might not have been true. | Identifiers: LCCN
2016006188 | ISBN 9780399546921 (hardback) | Subjects: |
CYAC: Fathers and daughters—Fiction. | Mothers and daughters—
Fiction. | Wealth—Fiction. | Arson—Fiction. | Terminally ill—
Fiction. | Classification: LCC PZ7.V25213 Fi 2017 | DDC [Fic]—
dc23 | LC record available at https://lccn.loc.gov/2016006188

Printed in the United States of America.   ISBN 9780399546921
10 9 8 7 6 5 4 3 2 1

Edited by Liza Kaplan. Design by Jennifer Chung.
Text set in 10.25-point Plantin Std.
This is a work of fiction. Names, characters, places, and incidents
either are the product of the author's imagination or are used
fictitiously, and any resemblance to actual persons, living or dead,
businesses, companies, events, or locales is entirely coincidental.

For my dad.

"*The Gods envy us. They envy us because we're mortal,*
because any moment could be our last. Everything is more
beautiful because we're doomed. You will never be lovelier
than you are now. We will never be here again."

—The Iliad, *via a movie in Hollywood,*
via a wall in Falmouth

Prologue

At my father's funeral, after everything, I lit a great big fire in his honor, built from stacked apple crates and broken furniture and pieces of a fallen-down tree. It towered over the scrubby piece of land I call the bonfire garden, and blazed, far enough from the house and too far gone to fight, against the fading afternoon. On the lawn below me, my family gulped for air in shock, like landed fish. They clawed at their own faces like Edvard Munch's Screamers, like meth-heads. Mourners poured from the house, designer-clad and howling, lit up like specters by the flames.

My stepfather, Lowell Baxter, aging pinup boy, one-time TV star, and current no-hoper, stood swaying, dazed and hollow-eyed, a man woken up in the wrong place after a long sleep. Hannah, my mother, crumpled onto the wet grass like a just-born foal in all her credit-card finery, her gorgeous face collapsing in a slow puncture. She clutched at her own clothes, sobbing violently, but she didn't bother getting to her feet. I doubt she could remember how, she was so weighted down with debt.

I could have filmed them, preserved their agonies for repeat viewings, but I didn't. I did what my best and only friend, Thurston, always told me. I savored the moment, because the moment was more than enough. I stood back and watched them suffer, feeding fistfuls of paper to the flames.

I wondered if they'd ever speak to me again. I've always longed for Hannah and Lowell to stop talking.

They didn't behave that way when it was my father in the furnace. Neither of them was sorry to see him go. Before the fire, there was a service for him at the crematorium. Ernest Toby Jones, one of a queue of waiting dead. Lowell worked the room in a tight suit, and Hannah wore big black sunglasses to hide her lack of tears, and shiny black high heels with red soles, same color as her lipstick. High-impact accessories are my mother's answer to big occasions, in place of actual feelings.

I couldn't stand the thought of Ernest lying in that box with the lid closed, all dark and lonely and gone. None of it made sense to me. I couldn't keep up. But like water putting out a lit match, the rest of the world closed over the fact of his absence and ran on. His hearse continued through everyday traffic. Cars behind him on the road tested their patience throughout his slow and stately journey to the grave. Only one old man, walking with a stick, stopped as the coffin navigated a roundabout and met my eye, and bowed his head politely to the dead.

Inside the chapel, a thin crowd spread itself out across the pews and tried to fill up the room. God knows who most of them were. They wore their dullest clothes and tuned their voices to the frequencies of sadness and loss. I sat on my own. I didn't want anything to do with them.

I stared down at Technicolor carpets, cheap knockoffs from *The Shining*, from a shut-down Las Vegas casino. I wanted to meet the person responsible and find out if they were joking, or color-blind, or just a fan of Stanley Kubrick films. I wanted to tell Thurston about them because he would get it and because, on that day of all days, I could have done with him there. And then I realized the carpets were chosen perfectly, because they took my mind off the elephant in the room, the rubbed-raw stump of what was missing, the lack of my father, the lack of Ernest, who was never ever coming back.

I didn't have him for long enough. That's the bare bones of it. I wasn't ready, once I'd found him, to let go.

"Do you want a song played?" I'd asked him, the week before. "When the curtains close, when your coffin goes through. Do you want a hymn or something?"

He thought about it for one waterlogged, morphine-soft moment.

"Harold Melvin and the Blue Notes," he said, and his voice sat like pea gravel in his mouth, sounded like mice scampering in a faraway attic. It took an age for the words to come out into the air. "'If You Don't Know Me by Now.'"

"*You will never, never, never know me,*" I sang, somewhere between laughter and tears.

Thurston threw a fake funeral once. He hired a hearse, and his uncle Mac drove it. I sat up front, and even though the coffin behind me was empty, it brooded, like something moody and alive, and I kept thinking there was someone else in the car. The windshield was thick with dead flies. Thurston walked ahead on the street at this slow, slow pace in a threadbare tailcoat and a tall black hat, a face like wet thunder, streaked with tears. It was a Sunday in the suburbs, Long Beach, out by Rossmoor. People were washing their cars and tidying their yards, and a gang of kids were riding their bikes in circles round a run-over cat. Uncle Mac just kept driving, slow as could be, following Thurston's lead with a great big smile plastered to his face. He didn't know what was going to happen next, and he liked it that way.

"I trust the boy," he said, "'cause he's a genius."

I wasn't about to argue with that.

The kids stopped circling, people stopped mowing and raking, and more still came right out of their houses, and everyone watched this funeral that wasn't theirs. You could see them wondering whose it was and what the hell it was doing on their street, on their weekend. And then when we had everyone's attention, Thurston reached into his jacket pocket at the exact same time I opened the car windows and cranked up the stereo, "It's Just Begun" by the Jimmy Castor Bunch. In one fluid movement, as the music gathered itself together, Thurston took four homemade pigment bombs and flung them out and down on the ground in front of him. He walked, and we followed, stately and respectful, through a thick and billowing cloud of color that swelled and rose and then drifted down, clinging to his tear-stained skin and his black clothes and to our somber, bug-stuck car. As we emerged from the color cloud and the song kicked in, Thurston started to dance. Not just foot tapping or finger clicking, not just any old thing. His whole body dipped and slipped and flowed like water through the music, the notes flinging him into the air and then low and wide across the ground until the smile on my face hurt just watching him, until I forgot to breathe. God, that boy could move.

Everybody but us was still, like we'd cast some kind of spell on them, like we'd stopped time but carried on traveling right through it. People stared. That's all they could do. It was the kind of funeral you'd long to have, the kind you'd see and then years later couldn't say if it was real or only a dream.

It was a moment, that's what it was. Thurston dreamed it up and handed it over to those Rossmoor people, for free. They had no idea what they were getting. They didn't know how lucky they were.

When Ernest's emptied body had hit temperatures close to 1600 degrees Fahrenheit and had been reduced to a shoe box full of strangely damp sand, cooling down for collection, I wished for him a great burst of sound and color, a celebration, a free dream. Instead everything was quiet and ordinary and shut down. There might have been a hymn, and people got up and shuffled out, looking only at the ground. We drove back in silence to his house

6

for refreshments and small talk, for gin-laced cocktails and tiny, harpooned sandwiches on the lawn. It would have been so much better with Thurston there to help me. I remember thinking that. It would have been something breathtaking and spectacular.

I wasn't wrong.

In the end, it was my best and last fire. I went out into the garden. The heat had dropped out of the sun and the light was leaving. I took a deep breath. I lit a match, put it calmly to the gas-soaked rags at the bonfire's skirts, and I waited.

And I only wished, with all my heart, that Ernest could have been around to see it.

One

Ernest must have given up on ever seeing me again when my mother called him at home out of the blue. We'd only been back in the country five days, stuck subletting a gloomy basement apartment with not enough windows. It was a Monday morning and it was raining. Ernest said if he'd drawn up a list of a thousand people it could possibly be, we wouldn't have made the bottom of it. We'd been gone more than twelve years. He'd quit thinking he'd find us a long time ago.

Hannah and Lowell had talked about it the night before. They'd talked of nothing else for days, in fact, since before we left home, how she was going to play it, what she was going to say. Turned out they'd been planning the whole thing for much longer. Lowell told her to act like nothing had happened, and I guess that's what she did.

"We're back," she said to Ernest, just like that, like we'd been away for the weekend.

A wormhole could have opened on the other side of the room and Ernest would have been less surprised, less terrified.

"Hannah?" He breathed her name into the receiver. "Is that you?"

I could hear his voice, stunned, small, and tinny through the back of the phone, like a man trapped in a cookie jar. I stayed close and listened. I'd never heard my real father speak before, not that I could remember anyway. He'd washed his hands of us a long time ago, and that was that.

"Yes, Ernest," my mother said, assessing her face in the mirror, smoothing out the lines around her mouth with her free hand, then letting go, facial time-travel, back and forth, back and forth. "It's me."

It must have stripped him right back to the bone, her sudden call, her carrying on like nothing had happened all those years. I didn't think about it then, but I do now, all the time.

"God, this place is a dump," she said, over his stunned silence. "*So* gray and *so* cold."

"Is Iris with you?" Ernest asked her.

She didn't answer him directly. It's one of the few things about Hannah you can always count on—her lack of generosity, her guaranteed refusal to give a person what they want. The question bounced off her, and she just moved right along.

"We've got some work with the BBC."

"News to me," I said under my breath, because as far as I knew, we'd been running from dwindling funds and a mountain of debt and other trouble, not headed toward a bright new future. Hannah slapped me on the back of the arm and gestured at me to zip it or get out.

"It's a really good move for us," she said, "apart from the weather."

"Why have you called, Hannah?" I heard him say. "What do you want?"

My mother has a special voice for deal making. It's sharp and flinty, like a rock face, like gritted teeth. She locks everything into a safe and then she opens her mouth. "Shall we meet?"

There was a pause, just quiet on the line like he was thinking about it. He wasn't exactly jumping at the chance.

"Why now?" he said.

"Don't you want to?" Hannah put her hand over the mouthpiece and hissed, "See?" like this was proof she'd always been right about him. I got ready to be rejected all over again. I hadn't been expecting anything different. It wasn't even that big a deal.

"It's not that," he said.

"So what is it?"

"I'd need you to come here."

I figured that was that. I was about to leave the room and get on with the rest of my Ernest-less life. Hannah told me once that Ernest lived alone in the middle of nowhere and that she'd never go back because it was just about the dullest place on earth, with no shops or Wi-Fi or bars or people or streets or houses. My mother was a fish out of water in a place like that, a bird of paradise in a cesspit.

"Just sheep," she'd said, "and grass. And Ernest," and she'd shuddered at the horror of it. "Never, ever again."

"Why's that?" she asked him now in an I'm-holding-all-the-cards, mountain-to-Mohammed, over-my-dead-body kind of way. "Why don't you come to London? I thought we could meet at the Royal Academy. You can buy me tea at Fortnum's, like you used to."

A trip like that was beyond him. Just getting out of bed was a half-hour operation, followed by a three-hour sleep. But we didn't know that yet.

"Bring Iris if you can," he said. "I'd really like to get another look at her before I'm gone."

"Another look?" I whispered. "What am I? A vase?"

"Gone?" she said, swatting me away. "Where are you going?"

"I'm sick," he told her.

"What's wrong with you?"

He paused. I could hear it. "Lung, liver, bone," he said. "Oh, and brain. I forgot to say brain."

He could have lied. He could have made something up, I suppose, but he gave it to her straight. He was dying.

I felt the base of my stomach drop out, just for a second, like it does on a roller coaster, when you're at the top and about to tip over and it's too late to change your mind and go back. Thurston was always looking for that feeling. He said he went after it because he could never tell if it was the tail end of excitement or the beginning of remorse. I said maybe it was both and wasn't that possible, and he said that was exactly why he liked me, precisely why we were friends.

Hannah's pupils deepened like wells, and she gripped the receiver harder, until her knuckles went white. She made the right noises, but they didn't match the look on her face.

"Oh God," she said. "How long have you got?"

"Hard to tell," I heard Ernest say. "Weeks, if I'm lucky."

"And how long have you known?"

12

"Not nearly long enough."

"And you're sure?"

"I'm sure, Hannah," he said. "It's over. I'm out."

I watched her wet her lips with the tip of her tongue, like she could taste something sweet. Hannah saw me watching and turned away. "She's sixteen, you know," she said, twirling at her hair with her fingers, sliding it past her teeth, checking for split ends. "Iris. Can you believe it?"

Ernest breathed for a bit, which sounded like someone walking on Bubble Wrap, and then he said, "There are things I've been hoping to give her. Family things. It would mean a lot, to be able to see her myself."

It didn't mean much to me one way or another, not back then. I was too busy working out how I was ever going to get home, worrying about how I was going to find Thurston. Family wasn't high on my list. Blood is no thicker than water, not when you've been on the other side of the Atlantic Ocean for most of your life, not when the one person you care about is still over there, and not talking to you, and you haven't had a chance to say sorry, or good-bye.

Hannah looked at me, all worked up and wide-eyed, but I just shrugged.

"What things?" she said, too fast if you ask me, too hungry.

13

"Just some paintings."

"*Just some paintings,*" she echoed through her Cheshire Cat smile.

"If she wants them."

"Oh, Iris is into her art," she drooled. "She'll want them."

"So bring her," he said. "Come and visit."

She used this pouting, sugar-soaked voice to shake him down. "And what do I get if I do? Are you going to make it worth my while?"

I was ashamed of her, honestly. I didn't know where to look. And at the same time, I thought maybe Ernest deserved to be played by her, that he'd made his own bed, after all. I definitely remember thinking about that.

"Let's talk about it when you get here," he said.

"*If* I get there." Hannah hardened up again. "Not *when*. I can't promise, Ernest. It's not a given. I can't just drop everything."

I wondered what it was she thought she was carrying, what it was she'd have to drop, apart from credit cards and cigarettes and gum.

There was a silence then. I heard the loose wet rattle of him sighing into the phone. Hannah counted with her fingers, slowly, for my benefit, and I realized she already knew how this would go. She winked at me, like we were in it together.

14

"You'll be rewarded," Ernest said. "You know how generous I can be."

"I do," she said.

"Come soon," he told her. "I don't have much time left."

When she put the phone down, she was glowing. She couldn't wait for Lowell to get back from his audition so she could tell him the good news. Everything about the way my mother moved around the room was different after that call, lighter, like she'd just mainlined a barrel full of hope.

I didn't want to go. I didn't feel like humoring him. The last thing I wanted was to be the centerpiece of an old man's guilt trip.

"This is good news, Iris," she said. "For both of us. Please don't try and spoil it."

"Good news how?"

"Your father," she told me, "was a very wealthy man."

"*Is*," I said. "You just got off the phone with him. He's not dead yet."

"Yes, OK." She dialed Lowell's number, pulled a face. "*Is*. But he'll be dead soon."

I laughed. "You look human," I told her, "but inside you've got to be part android."

"Don't give me that," she said. "You know he left us with nothing."

"You've told me many times."

"So don't waste your time sticking up for him. He's been a terrible father to you."

"And he's going to be a better one when he's dead? Is that it?"

Hannah hooked the phone between her jaw and her shoulder, and poured herself just an inch or two of vodka. Morning measures. Breakfast of Champions.

"Get what you can out of Ernest Toby Jones," she said. "That's my advice to you, free of charge."

Nothing is free of charge in my mother's world. She never gave a thing away without making somebody somewhere pay for it. I knew her well enough to know we weren't in this together, not for a second.

"Is that what you plan to do?" I asked her. "Get what you can?"

"You'll feel the same way," she said, "once you see the pictures he's got on his walls."

"What pictures?"

"Priceless ones," she said.

"Which artists?"

She waved the question away with a flip of her hand and rubbed her fingers and thumbs together, the way people do when they can smell money.

16

"Whatever," I said. "I'm not interested in how much they're worth."

"You will be," she said.

"And why's that?"

She smiled. "You think you're immune to the dollar," she said. "You think you're above all that, but you're not."

She knocked the vodka back with a quick snap of her head. I watched her swallow it, watched the mechanism working in her throat like rocks in a sack. Mother's little helper.

"To Ernest," she said, recalibrating her smile as the drink hit her bloodstream. "You and me and his millions are all he's got."

Two

Hannah and Lowell stayed up later than ever that night, getting reckless, lurching toward triple-strength cocktails and dancing around the living room. Neither of them had to be up for work in the morning. They probably thought they'd never have to work again. I could hear them talking about cruise ships and second homes in the South of France and film financing and plastic surgery. They were celebrating their sudden, soon-to-be fat fortune, counting their chickens, peaking too early, as usual.

I remembered the time Thurston and I talked about what we'd do with a vast, Forbes Top Ten Rich List, silly, unforgivable amount of money.

Change the world, Bill and Melinda Gates style.

Live on another planet, but only on weekends.

Get ten-dollar bicycles for four million of the world's poor.

Buy United Technologies (or Fox or Walmart or all three) and close them down.

"Give it all away to strangers," he said, "face-to-face, in random, life-changing acts of generosity."

"Set fire to it," I said, "and enjoy the look on my mother's face."

He said that if by some miracle I ever got that kind of rich, I should be sure to let him know, and that he would help me decide.

"You'll be the first person I call," I said, even though I knew he didn't have a cell phone and never would. Tracking devices, Thurston called them, and he refused to be tracked.

A fine principle, I told him, an interesting stand. Worse than useless, it turns out, when you're trying to find somebody, when you want to tell them where in the world you've disappeared to, when you need to see if they're anything like even halfway to OK. After we left in such a hurry, I realized I didn't even know where Thurston lived. I never went there. He never told me. It just didn't come up.

I rolled onto my side and pressed a pillow over my head to shut

Hannah and Lowell's noise out. I tried to think about Ernest. I'd only ever seen photos, one or two, of a serious, comb-haired, indoors sort of a guy, a bit of a geek, startled by the camera. They were yellowed and faded with age, those photos, like they came from a different time, like they had nothing at all to do with me. I wanted to feel something about him dying, I knew I should, but really he was no more than biology to me. We had nothing in common, unless you'd count a total lack of interest in each other. His silence my whole life kind of spoke for itself. I grew up hearing it, as loud as any of Hannah's yelling ever got to be.

I'd taken a couple of pills from my mother's well-stocked bathroom cabinet, and I lay there waiting for the day's sharp edges to blur into sleep. The sheets felt rough beneath me like thin cotton over sandpaper, and my pajamas twisted tight around my legs like a trap. I closed my eyes and imagined random objects in my bedroom bursting obligingly into flames, my very own tailor-made way to relax. It wouldn't work for everyone, but it sure as hell worked for me. Behind my eyelids, everything was torched and blasted with fire. My shoes smoldered, my alarm clock warped and melted, my bedding was ablaze. I felt like a superhero on a day off, like a plume of smoke, cloud-wrapped, buoyant. I couldn't move, but inside I was flying. The skin on my palms seethed and bubbled. I was a burning candle, I was a pool of hot wax and then I was gone.

Some days inside my head there is nothing but fire. Most nights I sleep deep inside its bright, fast blooms. I have longed for it in random places—the baths near our old apartment, the vacant Embassy Hotel on South Grand, that copse of pine and ash beyond Ernest's garden, the painted house downtown where my mother went to therapy for a while and left me in the waiting room, willing the fish to broil in their gravelly, weed-wrapped tank. My fingers itch constantly for the length and neck and strike of a match. My heart swells and soars at a column of smoke against the sky. I pine for the flame's lick, the sharp scorch in my lungs, the same way an addict pines for the needle. Thurston said once that I had the sweet moment of surrender all tangled up with love, and maybe he was right, but that didn't mean I knew the first thing about how to untangle them.

I tried to keep my fires small after we moved back here, small and secret. Hannah was watching me like a hawk, ready to ship me off to some correctional center or other, now that she could do it for free thanks to good old health care. I couldn't let her see me. I needed to be cleverer than that. A wastepaper basket, some old clothes, dry leaves, a length of rope, everything has its own flame. Everything burns at its own pace, with its own particular smoke and smell. I made fires every day because I had nothing better to do; little heaps of dry matter assembled and lit before breakfast, after lunch, behind buildings, on wastelands, on walkways and under bridges. I was fast and precise. I could start one in seconds, get up and walk away, my mind a little emptier, my breathing easier. Nothing got damaged, not by the small fires. They were actually pretty useful in their way, a kind of tidying up, an imposing of order and neatness on things. They didn't do any harm.

I was twelve when I lit my first real fire, and I was alone. I hid in a hollowed-out oak in a quiet dip in Griffith Park, dragging in gathered sticks and strips of bark like a worker ant. I was careful about building it. I took my time. I had a rolled-up old magazine of Hannah's in my back pocket for starting it—hungry-looking ladies with skinny jeans and tight smiles. I had to twist the pages just so—too loose and they'd flare out before the wood could catch, too much and they wouldn't burn at all. I'd watched Lowell do it often enough in the cramped, weed-choked yard of our apartment building. Now it was my turn.

I had only one match. I don't remember where I found it. I held it up and even I could see how small and pitiful it looked, how unlikely it was to start anything worth bragging about. I breathed in and ran the match across the gritted bottom of my shoe, felt the stroke of it, heard the little pucker of air when it caught. And then I lifted it, burning, into view. It was thrilling to me. It was the start of everything, right there in my hand.

I shielded the tiny flame, moved it slowly so its own breeze didn't put it out, and then I touched it to the twisted paper. The smiling ladies writhed and blackened, and the smoke rose in a rainbow of grays. When the fire leapt up, I felt its heat, warped and dancing in front of me like liquid, like magic. I didn't know a flame could burn so many shades. Every color in the world was in that fire, and watching it burn was the biggest, boldest feeling. I've never felt it again like the first time, not quite like that.

I got out of that hollow when I had to, when the heat and the smoke made it hard to see and harder to breathe. I stayed low and made sure there was nobody around. My hands on the ground were covered with dust and ash. They looked like statues' hands. I moved away fast and then I stopped to watch the smoke from my fire rolling fat and dark as a storm cloud.

At the top of the park, from the observatory, you can see way out over the endless fume-hung map of grid streets and thin trees and squat tower blocks and lit highways, as far as the horizon—

farther. My fire was a little insult to all that, something wild in plain view of the city. It felt like a door had swung open, like I'd been kept in an airless room all this time and finally I could breathe. I didn't want to get caught, I knew I should hurry, but it was like trying to run in a dream. Bright sparks and flakes of charred leaf floated down through the blue behind me, light as feathers, and the flames licked and snapped like a dragon, biting clean through solid wood.

I moved clumsily toward the subway, until I couldn't see the smoke, but all the same I knew it was there. Once I was on the train, I spotted a boy, pale and dark-haired and skinny, older than me, fifteen it turned out, standing in the middle of the car, and he was holding up a handwritten sign and looking at me like he wanted to make sure I saw it. It read WHAT HAVE YOU DONE? I went red hot and looked at my dust-covered shoes.

"*Psst*," he said, and I looked up again, and the other side read WAS IT WORTH IT? DID IT FEEL GOOD? and I nodded and looked straight at him, and we smiled.

That was Thurston. That's how we met. On the subway, eight stops from Griffith to home, he showed other people the same sign, and I watched him. He held it up and waited for someone to notice—an old lady, a shifty-looking guy, a girl with her hair tied up high on her head, earrings swinging—and the whole time, he stayed looking at me.

I loved it. I'm telling you, nobody had made me smile like that my whole goddamn life. I got off at my stop because I had to, but I didn't want to leave, and when I waved at the boy, he winked at me and smiled right back.

Back home, Hannah and Lowell were out, but they'd be back soon, crashing through the door and trampling on my quiet with their verdicts on the relentless heat, the price of everything, and the vital overall importance of their day. Much better, this peace, this alone time, this thinking about the boy on the subway, this picturing my fire. As it burned out there in the park, I washed my hands and face, scrubbed the dirt from under my nails, pulled off my clothes and hid them under the bed. The smell of fire was still in my shirt, sweet and black and smoky. I put my face in the sleeve at the bend in my elbow, and I breathed.

I was hooked right then, on both of them, the boy and the fire. I don't mind owning up to that.

In London, four years later and half a world away, I'd have dreamt about Thurston if I could. I'd have traded him for fire, but even in my sleep, I couldn't find him.

In the morning, the noise of the real world descended like a net and caught me in it. Somewhere a truck was backing up, a car door slammed. I could hear Lowell making coffee, banging cupboard doors, and sweating out his hangover. I felt the weight of my own body like gravity, pinning me down in the wrong place, in the wrong city, on this bed.

I opened my eyes, and everything was the same as the night before, unfamiliar, intact, and unspoiled. No plain blue still-as-a-picture California sky but something lower and rolling and cold. No posters on the walls like in my old room, no piles of clothes or comic books, just unpacked boxes. No Thurston throwing stuff at my window, waiting on the corner so we could begin another day. No heaps of ash, no charred and twisted remains, just carpet and plaster and metal, and a father I'd never met and didn't want to meet, dark on the horizon like a storm. I couldn't have been more disappointed.

Three

My mother has four main stories she likes to tell: the edited highlights of her modeling career (who said what, who touched her where), her disastrous marriage to Ernest (no redeeming features), her many visits to Europe (ditto—Paris is littered with dog shit apparently, Venice is a rip-off, and Florence is a bore), and the time she spilled a bowl of soup at the American ambassador's house in Regent's Park. If I hadn't seen it for myself now and again, the odd moment of vulnerability, the occasional spark of something like love, I wouldn't believe she had a heart in her body. She never talks about anything real. She never gives herself away. It's like her life started at twenty-one, like nothing happened before that was worth mentioning.

"Maybe it didn't," Ernest said to me once. "Maybe things were awful." And it made sense, I suppose, of the way she drinks and thinks of everything as a fight, and grabs hold of the day like it's a sheer drop and if she doesn't dig her nails right in, she'll fall.

Back home, whenever we had people over, Hannah would prep herself under the lights the minute the doorbell rang. She'd roll out variations of her four stories while Lowell pretended to cook deli-bought meals from scratch, throwing his head back when he laughed, rattling pans. There was no trace of our usual cook-your-own-pizza-and-stay-out-of-sight arrangement. They didn't work their way through a bottle of vodka in old T-shirts if there were guests in the house. They hid the TV in a cupboard and acted like we spent our spare time holding hands and listening to recordings of T. S. Eliot reading "The Waste Land." They enjoyed putting on a show. I guess it made them both feel as if they were working.

My job was to pour the drinks and play it like we were your dream family, like really the best of friends. We couldn't keep it up for long. Four minutes was about the limit. If we strayed into five, one or the other of us got bored or cranky and had to leave the room.

I used to think it was a miracle that anyone believed them. But people believe what they see. And mostly they see whatever is put in front of them, if it's in their interests to do so. If someone gave you a fat stack of money and told you to spend it, you'd probably think the money was real. If they handed you a diamond and said it was worth as much as a house, you'd want it to be true, you'd want to get as much as possible out of it.

The first and only time Thurston met Hannah and Lowell, he showed up dressed as a girl. More precisely, he showed up dressed as Hannah, wearing clothes he must have taken from her closet some time before, when I wasn't looking.

Lowell answered the door.

"Your friend's here," he said to me.

"What friend?"

"Charlotte."

I didn't look up. "I don't know anybody named Charlotte."

"Well, she's here," he said, "and she's asking for you."

This girl came into the room, all long legs and lipstick and fingernails. Beautiful, flawless, just Hannah's type, the kind of girl I avoided like the plague, who wouldn't notice if she tripped over me in the street in her Manolo Blahniks.

"It's Charlie," she said, "remember?" Stretching out toward me, all grabby and polished, like some kind of sisterhood reunion. I looked down at her hands, and I saw the little star tattoo at the base of the left thumb, and it was only then that I realized it was Thurston.

"Oh God. *Charlie!*" I said. "So sorry."

Charlie was bespoke, made-to-measure perfect for Hannah and Lowell to fall in love with—an Orange County girl, drowning in labels, with money in her veins and parents who did, "Oh, you know, something in the movies." She dropped names in a way that made the sweat break out on Lowell's forehead, always the first name twice, to show how well she knew them.

"Leo, Leo DiCaprio's got one of those," she said, pointing to our crappy vintage-style blender. "Cate, Cate Blanchett would just *love* how you've done this wall."

"She's got style," Hannah said, watching her own skirt stretched tight over Thurston's narrow hips.

"Good manners," Lowell said, doing the thoughtful movie-star clench with his jaw, already wondering whether she had a crush on him, already working out how to get in with her people.

It didn't for a second occur to them that this was a piece of on-and-off-homeless, skinny-male white trash from the uglier side of town, graffiti maestro, street artist, performance poet, and pickpocket, with a mild criminal record (trespassing, jaywalking, vagrancy) and no sway whatsoever in the Hollywood Hills.

30

Even if I had told them right then, I don't think they would have believed it.

Just the week before, Thurston had strung a huge banner from the top of the Ocean Palms building, hand-stitched in letters more than six feet tall, FROM UP HERE WE ARE ALL NOBODIES. That wouldn't have meant a thing to Hannah and Lowell. There was nothing in that for them.

"Can I take your daughter out tonight?" Charlie asked, and they looked surprised as hell that someone so spectacular might know me, but they said yes, of course they said yes.

Thurston kissed them each on both cheeks as we headed out, and they didn't feel the stubble underneath his smooth skin, didn't notice the bitten-down nails behind the false ones.

"I can't believe you just did that," I said once we had closed the door behind us.

"No big deal," he said. "Everyone here is faking it."

"I suppose."

"How the hell," he asked me, taking my arm on the stairs, "does anyone walk in these shoes?"

We stopped at the bottom of the stairwell in my building. Thurston had stashed his clothes there, his baggy black T-shirt and ancient jeans. When he came out looking like Thurston

31

again, I thought he was a hundred times more beautiful than Charlie, but I kept my mouth shut.

He grinned. "They loved me, right?"

"You were perfect," I told him. "How could they not?"

"Jeez," he said, "your parents are easy to please."

Charlotte never appeared again. A while later, Hannah and Lowell asked me what happened to her.

I was reading about a sinkhole that had opened up out of nowhere underneath a man's house and swallowed his bed with him still in it.

"I haven't seen her," I said.

"Why doesn't that surprise me?"

"I get it," I told her. "Too good for me, right?"

"Such great potential," Hannah said, like she'd know.

"I wanted to have her parents over this weekend," Lowell said.

I suppose they wanted to believe I'd had a friend with connections, that it might almost make me somebody.

"She died," I told them, and I didn't care if they bought it or not. "She moved away."

Lowell's face hovered somewhere around shock at the further thinning of his address book, and Hannah said, "Well, which is it?"

"Both," I said. "But not in that order."

They didn't bother to argue.

Gullible works both ways. Tricking people requires their full co-operation, and people are lazy. They're happy to have the wool pulled over their eyes, because everything else is just plain hard work.

Four

I call my mother Hannah because she told me to. When I was about seven, she said it was time to stop being a baby and start using her real name.

"Otherwise," she said, turning to enjoy her reflection from behind, "the older you get, the more you'll age me."

She is a beauty. I have to give her that. Tall and dark and glossy, like some kind of racehorse, with legs and curves that people feel the need to stare at in the street. We are nothing alike.

I am plain-looking, skinny and flat-chested and small, and it suits me. I live in thrift-shop jeans and secondhand sweaters because they come in under budget and under the radar, and they're just easy. I cut my hair short like a boy for the same reason. I've banked myself plenty of time and money by never caring too much what I look like. I think my day is about four hours longer than Hannah's without all the grooming in it. It's actually quite liberating, not giving a shit. What am I missing out on exactly—makeup, brand anxiety, and crippling self-doubt about shoes? Big deal. Poor me. If I were in charge, mirrors would be for making sure there's nothing stuck in your teeth or sticking out of your nose or tucked into your jeans, nothing more. I'm not going to start staring into one and wishing I were different.

I used to wonder if that was why Thurston chose me, because I was unremarkable, because I'd be useful to him that way. Every hustler needs an invisible friend.

One day we were making him a mask out of old, broken sunglasses, sticking the smashed lenses onto a plain latex face, so that when people looked at him, all they would see were reflections of themselves.

"I like you, Iris," he said, holding it up in front of his face, pulling the strap to the back of his head. "You are exactly yourself."

I was fourteen. I'd known Thurston on and off for two years, and he was the only thing I had worth knowing. It was the nicest thing he could have said to me. My smile just about exploded, reflected at hundreds of angles by his mirrored mosaic of a face.

• • •

Hannah and Lowell think I am determined to be ugly. They think my attitude is aimed at them, out of spite. It's beyond them that somebody would go a whole day without looking in the mirror. They wouldn't dream of leaving the house without a layer of light-reflecting foundation and an accessory with a three-figure price tag. Looking good is the actual bedrock of their moral code. Presentation is ethics to them, which is why they bought me the dress. Hannah threw it down on my bed like a gauntlet, this loud patterned thing with a belt. I avoided it, walked around it like you would a patch of vomit in the street. I took a shower, pulled on yesterday's clothes, and went downstairs for breakfast.

It was Saturday, the weekend after Hannah called Ernest and agreed to bring me (I think) for a price. I could see they'd been shopping. Lowell was pacing the kitchen in a stiff pale suit that made him look like a rectangle, like a man in a cardboard box. Hannah had on a mink silk top and a skirt so tight I wasn't sure she could move. I think she had to cross her legs the whole time to fit into it. They looked like they'd just stepped out of a shop window. I wondered how many hours the two of them had spent fantasizing about the scene at Ernest's deathbed and the muted, elegant, expensive clothing they would suddenly be able to afford. I wanted to put a match to the hem of Hannah's skirt and set it on fire, drop a hot coal down the neck of Lowell's jacket and watch it swallow up the fabric like a black hole.

"Morning," I said.

Hannah leaned against the kitchen counter, nursing a cigarette for breakfast. My mother often smokes instead of eating. She'd sell you a diet book about it if someone would let her. Her blown smoke bloomed in the bands of sunlit air that striped the kitchen, vanishing in its shadows, expanding to fill the room.

"Kiddo," Lowell said, like every morning, in his faked transatlantic drawl. "Nice of you to show up."

"Where's the dress?" Hannah asked, and I poured myself some cornflakes before I told her it was still in the package.

"Aren't you going to wear it?"

"Nope. You should definitely take it back."

Hannah pointed at me with her smoking hand, and an inch of ash fell soundlessly onto the soft suede toe of her brand-new shoe.

"Well, you can't go like that."

"Why not?" I looked down at myself. "I'm always like this."

"Lowell," she said, still pointing. "Talk to her."

Lowell's jacket was too starched and too big, like the cardboard box was trying to swallow him whole.

"It's a great dress," he said, "really on-trend," as if his opinion mattered, like that would change my mind. He talked like one of the girls at my old high school. I thought he'd fit right in there, simpering over labels in the hallways, bitching in the lunch line about boys.

"So you wear it," I told him with my mouth full. "Help yourself."

"Just once," Hannah said through gritted teeth.

"Just once what?" I asked her, but I knew the answer. She wanted me to fit seamlessly into the picture-perfect lifestyle she had filling the space in her head, to stop being difficult and strange, to dress up and shut up and play along. We stared at each other. She looked away first. I always win that game.

Lowell had already given up and gone back to his magazine. There were lots of people in it he'd stood quite close to over the years. Things were happening. Men more successful than him were starting to lose their hair.

"Let her wear what she likes, Hannah," he said. "A dying man is going to have other things on his mind."

My mother put her hands together in prayer at the word

dying and looked up past the burst radiator stains on the ceiling.

"God knows," she said, "we could all do with a bit of good luck right now."

I asked her where she thought God filed that kind of prayer, the please-harm-others-for-my-benefit kind, and she ignored me. "In a box marked DAMNED, probably," I said, "in a whole archive called *Be Careful What You Wish For.*"

"What do you care?" she asked me. "You're an atheist, aren't you? You don't believe in God."

"Humanist," I said. "There's a world of difference."

Thurston made a God box once. It was like a mailbox, with a slot, and he wrote on it PRAYERS ANSWERED. You were supposed to write your prayer and mail it. That was the idea. He left it for four days on the corner of Westwood and La Conte, near the university. When he went back, there was some trash in it, a couple of crushed cans, a banana peel and half a bagel. There was some angry stuff about blasphemers and the wrath of the Lord. But mostly there were wish lists, money troubles, exam results, job opportunities, and a couple of lonely hearts. My favorite one was written in pencil on a square of pink paper—THAT THIS BOX IS FOR REAL.

My cornflakes were stale and chewy. The milk was going bad. New outfits aside, it hadn't been a good month moneywise, again. I knew that was why we were doing this. Hannah had slot-machine eyes, especially now that she knew Ernest was on his way out. She was desperate to get there and clean up. Beneath the surface she trembled with it, like a greyhound on the starting blocks, like a size-zero bull at a gate.

"When did you last see him?" I asked.

"When did he abandon us? I don't know. Thirteen years? Fourteen? Maybe twelve. When was it, Lowell?"

Lowell shrugged. "Beats me."

I pushed my bowl away. "And why are you all dressed up, exactly? What's with that?"

"We've got to look like we're doing well," she said, pinching a strand of tobacco from the surface of her tongue without smudging her lipstick, the same smashed-cherry color as her nails. "I don't want him thinking we need his money."

As if a new outfit could do that. As if a throw-up dress or a stomach-bug-brown suit would hide our flock of overdrafts, a good silk blouse erase the sly and bottomless need from our eyes.

"Why do you care what he thinks?" I said.

"We're going in there with our heads held high," said Lowell.

"And coming out with our hands full, right? To the victor go the spoils?"

I didn't want a thing from Ernest. I didn't want to know him. I thought they should go without me. I had my eye on a clean conscience and the place to myself. I'd exercise control, build a fire in the grate, and feed it kindling so it stayed small but never went out. I'd write letters to Thurston at all the addresses I could think of—the bar where his uncle Mac drank, the record store he liked in Echo Park, everyone at my old apartment building. I'd track him down so I could tell him what had happened, where on planet earth I was. I'd leave the lights off and the blinds down, be nothing but a glowing, empty house. I wasn't interested in helping Ernest feel better about himself. I didn't have room to play suck-up to my sick old stranger of a father in exchange for what he might be leaving me in his will.

"Do I have to come with you?" I said.

Hannah smashed out her dead cigarette on a plate like it had done something to offend her. She lit a fresh one and pulled on it so hard her cheeks caved in and I thought she'd smoke the whole thing down in one breath. She saw me, and I knew what she was thinking. Gone were the days when Little Miss Arson could be left alone in the house. There wasn't enough insurance money in the world that could pay for that.

"Yes, you have to come," she said. "It's *you* he's interested in."

"Yeah," I said. "*Now.*"

Her fingers drummed hard on the counter and she declined, as usual, to answer the question. "It's not optional. We're not negotiating."

"Think of it as a vacation," Lowell suggested, the shoulders of his suit rising up for no good reason to meet his ears, his right cuff already streaked with butter. "You can explore the garden. You can bring your bike."

I looked at him. "What am I? Eight?"

"God forbid we're there long enough for a bike ride," Hannah said.

Lowell stuck with it. "You can walk, or swim in the river. Maybe he's got a boat."

"An Outward Bound vacation in a dying man's house?" I said. "Nice. Sensitive."

Hannah smiled coldly at me.

"Let's be honest," I told her. "You're going fishing, and I'm the bait."

"It's remote," she said. "It's isolated. He's got acres of land,

and woodland. It's a great place for a fire. You could light ten of the damn things out there, and nobody would even notice."

I didn't look up. I kept my eyes on my cereal bowl. "Who else is going to be there?"

"Just us," Hannah said. "Ernest's been on his own for years."

"How do you know?" I said.

She bent toward her reflection in the side of the toaster. It was warped and squat and gauzy. "I just do," she said, baring her teeth to check for stains. "Trust me."

My chair legs scraped loudly against the floor as I got up. "Why the hell would I start doing that?"

I rinsed my bowl in the sink. Through the window, I could see next door's cat lurking on the fence by the bird feeder, waiting to take one out midflight with a swipe of its paw.

It was the start of the summer. I had plans.

Hannah played with her lighter, grinding the flint back and forward with her thumb, holding the gas down, looking right at me over the flame.

"You think he's really at death's door?" I said, and (may God forgive me), "Will it be quick?"

"Fingers crossed." She smiled, and Lowell got up to start packing the car.

Five

We drove out of the city toward Ernest on a bright clear day. He said he woke up to the dry powder blue of the sky, and he knew we were coming. The Severn Bridge looked like the entrance to heaven in an old film I'd seen about a pilot who'd rather not die yet, thanks all the same, because he'd just met a nice lady and only recently started to enjoy himself. The service station on the other side where we stopped for coffee looked like the mouth of hell.

Later, much later, I told Ernest this. We were playing cards. He said I played poker like a professional. Apparently, I shuffle like a dealer.

"And by the way," he told me, "it's only in a film you

can decide not to die because your life has taken a sudden turn for the better."

I smiled, and kissed him on the forehead, and fanned the whole deck of cards out with one snap of my hand.

It was Thurston who showed me how to handle cards. He knew hundreds of tricks. He had this one where the card you chose would end up ripped in half in your back pocket, and he wouldn't ever tell me how it was done. "Magic" was all he said whenever I asked him. He said his uncle Mac taught him but I knew that was a lie because I once saw Mac try to shuffle a deck, and it was like he was doing it with his feet. By then I knew that Uncle Mac wasn't even his uncle, just some guy he'd met at a hostel, just another stray like me.

I thought about Thurston in the car all the way to Ernest's place. I remembered the look on people's faces when he pulled that card trick, the wonder, like he'd given them just what they'd been hoping for, like they were kids again just for a second, until they leaned in toward him and said, "How?"

Partly, I was glad he'd never told me. It would have ruined it, probably, to know. And I'm not saying that Thurston knew everything. Just that the things he told me were worth telling. And that he knew me. I couldn't say that about anyone else.

45

• • •

Four hours after we left home, we drove onto Ernest's property like tourists, suitcases piled up in the back, shopping bags and a black collapsible bicycle crowding at the windows to get out.

"If he's dead already, it all stays in the car," Hannah said.

I opened my window, which was tinted and stole the color from everything, like driving in black and white. The house was a warm golden yellow in the sun, tall with dark latticed windows and narrow brick chimneystacks. Lowell turned the car on the gravel driveway, and it scuttled over the stones like a roach. To our left was a copper beech hedge, the color of old coins, to our right a view of the vivid green garden through an iron gate in the wall. The wind moved in the leaves, and I could hear bird-song, and music coming from somewhere inside. I tried to picture someone lying upstairs in a darkened room, listening to a violin concerto, reeking of decay and disinfectant while we swooped in to stake our claim. I wondered if he heard the growl of our tires on his gravel, the beat of our wings.

"Look out, Ernest," I said. "Here come the vultures."

Lowell braked too hard, and the bike caught me on the side of the head with a punch.

"Ow!" I said.

Hannah retouched her makeup, pressed her lips together. "Be quiet, Iris. If you haven't got anything nice to say, then don't say anything at all."

I wanted to ask if, under those rules, any of us might ever speak again, but I kept my mouth shut.

Ernest wasn't dead, not yet. But he wasn't on his doorstep to meet us, either. Lowell brought the car to a halt and frowned into his rearview mirror. Birds scattered and resettled at the tops of trees, and the front door stayed shut, as if nobody was home. Hannah balled her hands into fists and took an in-breath that didn't seem to end. Lowell passed her a paper bag, and she breathed into it in quick little sips and flapped her spare hand back and forth in front of her face.

"Are you hyperventilating?" I asked. I'd never seen anyone do that in real life before.

She let out a high-pitched whine like a steam kettle.

"Stay calm," Lowell told her, reshaping his Superman kiss-curl with one finger. "We're in the homestretch."

"Yeah," I said, "maybe he's kicking it right this minute. Cling to that hope."

Truth is, I felt pretty anxious myself. My head was full of white noise, and I couldn't sort one sound from another, like everything was demanding to be heard at once, like I'd been turned inside out and exposed to the loud air. I guess I didn't expect to feel normal, though. It's not every day you get to meet the dad you never had.

Lowell and my mother clamped iron smiles onto their faces, and we got out, slamming the doors behind us. I turned my back on the house and looked out over the garden, across the fields, toward the woodland and the distant, shadowed hills. I breathed. Some species of tree are specially adapted to withstand and encourage fire. Some rely on it for their survival, to ensure their domination over other species, and to clear the soil and canopy for new growth. Trees look like their own shadows when they're burning. Flames fan out and eat up a hillside, way quicker than you'd think. Hannah was right. I could light fires out here, and no one would even know about it. It made me feel better, knowing that.

The front door swung open just as Hannah and Lowell reached it. The nurse must have run down as soon as she saw us.

"Welcome," she said. "Do come in."

Hannah and Lowell acted like they hadn't seen her. They knew how to treat staff, how to exploit a potential VIP situation

48

with disdain and to their own advantage. They'd learned that, at least, in LA, if nothing else. I caught up and followed them in, met the nurse's eye, tried to say in a smile that I was sorry about them and that I wasn't the same. I wasn't sure if she got it.

The square entrance hall had deep tall windows and a high-backed chair drawn up to the fireplace. The walls were washed gray, and on the dull stone floor, a thin bright yellow rug marked the pathway to the staircase, like the sun's pathway on the sea. I thought my shoes would leave marks on it, but they didn't.

Ernest might have had only minutes to live, but we still took our time. We had to check on the state of the art before we checked on him. First, Hannah wanted to show us the Joan Miró in the old kitchen, the Chagall lithographs and the Braque in the hall. She went all weak-kneed at the Picasso prints and the Modigliani in the dining room. My mother had the uncanny ability to forget even the most significant things, but when it came to Ernest's worth, her memory was clear as crystal.

"I had that valued years ago," she said to Lowell behind her hand, whispering. *"Over four million."*

Lowell put his hand on her arm and gave it an imagine-what-it's-worth-now squeeze.

They reminded me of a couple I saw at a gallery once. The

49

woman was wearing silver jeans, I remember, and the sound of the man's boots on the gallery floor was like gunshots, shouting look-at-me, look-at-me, look-at-me. They wanted to buy a painting. They didn't even care which one. They just stood in front of the brightest and the loudest and said, "How much?"

I thought of them while Hannah and Lowell grinned up at the Modigliani.

"Tip of the iceberg," she said, beaming at Lowell like she'd swallowed a torch.

However rotten their core, I have to admit he and my mother make a stunning couple and a damn good entrance. I watched them getting into character on the way up the stairs, walking with their shoulders back and their stomachs sucked in, shutters down on their eyes and catwalk sneers on their faces. It was like Fashion Week had arrived. The mannequins, Thurston used to call them, the rare times they came up in conversation; mannequins one and two. As in,

Thurston: Will mannequin one let you stay out that late?

Me: She won't even notice.

Thurston: What does mannequin two do all day?

Me: Mirror work, mainly.

We let the nurse show us the way, but we could have found

the room ourselves by following its sweet-sharp, metallic, medical stench to the second floor. It smelled pretty terrible in there. At the door, my mouth dried up and all the bones in my spine started singing. I'd have run away if I could, if it wasn't already too late.

Ernest was propped on a few extra pillows in his sparse, stone-colored bedroom, kind of sitting up when we came in. I felt white hot when I looked at him. I was half drowning in pins and needles, top to bottom, but I didn't take my eyes off him, not once.

Lowell shook his hand too hard, pumping it like a man trying to get water from a dried-up well. It's his audition handshake, two-handed, the one that goes with unnerving amounts of eye contact and exposed teeth. Somebody somewhere must have told him it was a good one, and he has tried, once or twice, to teach it to me. Ernest yelped a little when it started up and then he held on tight and brought the thing to a stop, like a galloping horse. Somewhere in his head I swear Lowell was Gary Cooper, or John Wayne, just for as long as that handshake. I thought Ernest's shoulder might dislocate. I thought his arm might snap clean off.

"Hello, old chap," Lowell said, the country house vibe already seeping into his language. "Great to see you."

He looked so healthy next to Ernest it was almost an insult. Lowell's teeth are toilet-bowl white. His eyebrows are plucked.

He has shiny Ken-doll hair, not a strand out of place. He is tanned and well moisturized, still a catch. The carcass looks good, but inside there is nothing but air. If you punctured Lowell Baxter with a pin, he would shrivel to nothing, loud and aimless like a balloon.

Ernest didn't speak. I guess dying people don't really care for small talk. It's not that they're more honest; I just don't think they have the energy or the time.

My mother stood behind Lowell, tapping her foot, and when he stepped back, she moved in, smiling too hard, like something sweet had stuck her teeth together. She bent to brush her cheek against Ernest's, and her arms slid around his neck like snakes.

"Ernest, darling," she drawled, the words spooling from her mouth like cold syrup. "How are you feeling?"

She didn't need to ask. You could see how he was. There was nothing but sickness in that room, with its drawn curtains and watering eyes and thinning skin. Ernest looked about twice his age, like if you held him up to the light, you'd see straight through.

Hannah tried to ditch her gloating expression, but it stuck to her face like the wind had changed. "I hope you're not in too much pain," she purred, stroking the front of his vest like a cat fixing to climb the curtains. Jesus, she was so damn obvious.

I stood in the doorway and let myself look back along the hall so I didn't have to watch any more. Through a half-open door, I saw a bright room with books piled on tables and curtains lifting in the breeze and a sofa in front of a cold fire. I'd have been happier in there—anywhere but here, probably, seeing all this. Next thing I knew, Hannah pulled me right into the room and pushed me toward him.

"Here's Iris," she said, like I was a clause in their contract, the package she'd been paid to deliver.

Ernest reached for my hand with his candle-wax fingers and I steeled myself and let him take it. His palm was damp and cold against my skin.

"Hello," I said, and my voice shook, my whole body hummed with the high-level strangeness of it all.

Later, Ernest said his larynx felt like a wood chipper. Great branches of thought passed through it and came out as nothing but dust. Here I was, and his damn voice wouldn't work. He smiled, he said, because that's all he could do, and there wasn't a word on earth good enough for him to use anyway.

I was all set to feel angry or sad or bewildered, and I think I was all of those things, and more. When Ernest smiled, the creases on his face stacked like towels in a showroom, like pieces of a puzzle.

How many times do you have to smile to carve such deep lines in your cheeks? Ten thousand? One million? If a person spends twenty years of their life asleep, how many weeks of it do they spend smiling? How much does that vary, from the saddest to the happiest life? How could this man have turned his back on me? These are the things I was thinking the first time I saw his face. How the hell could he have left me so alone?

Ernest was marooned on the white-pillowed island of his bed, with Hannah and Lowell swimming around him in ever-tightening circles like sharks, and he clung on to me like I was the only one who could help him. I didn't know how to feel about that. I tried to let go of his hand, but he wouldn't let me. I told myself this was my father, my real-life flesh-and-blood dad, but I had no idea what that actually meant. What use was flesh and blood you'd never been allowed to know?

Spending time with Thurston, I'd gotten used to that edge-of-a-drop feeling, like it was a good thing. He was always pulling stunts, winding things up and seeing which way they went. Like when he stood at the mall in Lakewood in a suit pinned thick, collar to ankle, with ten-dollar bills (some of them real, most of them made with a scanner) shouting "FREE MONEY" over and over again like some garbage-truck *Wizard of Oz* scarecrow.

My job was to wait for the reaction, to watch and remember—no filming, no recording allowed, just as a witness. Other people filmed him. There were more than enough phones in the place for that. At first people flowed around where he stood, avoiding him like a rock in the river, and then somebody reached out. I remember the first hand, and then all of a sudden, they were like bees to honey, like locusts, and I couldn't see Thurston at all until they'd stripped his suit bare and he was left there, spun and dazed and smiling, clean as a picked field. Afterward he said it wasn't about the money, it was the moment, the story they got to tell. It was for the look on people's faces when they said, "You're kidding. That happened for real?"

Sometimes the most exciting part was the waiting.

At Ernest's house that first day, I told myself I knew my way around the what-happens-now better than anyone else in that room. Thurston might not have been there to help me, but I could hear him anyway, telling me to breathe, and sit back, and not be too angry, or afraid, and just let it come.

The nurse shifted in the corner.

"Who *is* that?" Hannah asked.

Ernest didn't stop looking at me.

"Lisa," he whispered in a voice like dry straw. "Or Dawn."

"It's Dawn, Mr. Jones," she said.

"And who is Dawn, please?" Hannah showed her teeth in place of a smile.

"Dawn is the day," Ernest mumbled.

She smiled. "I'm one of the nurses. There are two of us looking after him. I do the day shift and Lisa does the nights. Oh, and Jane comes in to cook. She's been cooking for Mr. Jones for—"

"How charming," Hannah interrupted, her face pinched, her voice stretched tight like a twisted rag. She sighed, already bored, and looked out of the high windows at the cloud-washed, Turner-painting view. Lowell hovered with his hands at his sides, clenching his lantern jaw, rocking on his feet in that suit, waiting for her next instruction. Ernest closed his eyes.

Whole continents must have shifted. Glaciers formed. The land must have pressed together into mountains before he opened them again, and squeezed my hand, and said, "I'd know you anywhere. Isn't morphine the damnedest thing?"

"We'll stay a couple of days," Hannah said, because she reckoned that was all Ernest had left. "Go and get your things from the car," she told me. "I take it nothing around here has changed, Ernest? Iris, you have the yellow room. Lowell, we'll have the blue."

"Lowell?" said Ernest.

Hannah and Lowell stopped moving. They stopped dead for less than a second, like a break in transmission, but I noticed it still. The nurse cleared her throat and half put her hand up to speak.

"The blue room's Lisa's," she said. "I'm in the yellow."

My mother looked her up and down. "You're *living* here?"

"Yes," she said.

"Dawn is the day," I repeated. "And Lisa is the night."

"So we'll take the green room, then. Iris can go in the attic."

"Whatever," I said.

Lowell left quickly, ahead of her. I didn't move, not yet. Ernest was still holding on to my hand. It was uncomfortable. He was pinching me. I wanted so badly to be out of there.

"Hannah," he said.

She stopped in the doorway and turned back toward him. She has great hair, my mother. It swings and bounces and falls, shining like an oil slick. She works hard at keeping it moving at all times. If she wrote a résumé, she'd have to add it to her list of skills.

"Yes?" she said, and I swear, for no longer than a heartbeat, something in her eyes was soft and kind and open. Then it was gone.

Everything Ernest was really thinking, he must have flattened and folded like a car in a crusher, and crammed into the quick

57

look he gave her, like a library stored on the head of a pin. I must have blinked. Otherwise, I'm sure I'd have seen it. He'd have given himself away.

"Thank you," he said, a pearl of politeness after a lifetime of eating grit.

His mouth sounded as dried out as sea sponge; his eyelids looked heavy as lead.

"Lowell," he said, looking straight through me.

"Do you want me to get him?" I said.

Ernest smiled and shook his head. "Lowell and Hannah and Iris."

I looked at the nurse.

"Don't worry," she said. "He's tired now. He'll brighten up later."

He closed his eyes, and for a second or two, he seemed to think he was in the garden, flapping at insects and muttering about the lavender. He held on still to my hand, and the nurse kept busy in the corner, folding things, counting pills, making notes on a chart. The way Ernest must have seen it, Hannah had come storming through the long grass toward him in her heels, then the long grass became the floorboards of his room and he was in bed again, not outside, and she was glaring at us.

"What are you still doing standing there?" Hannah said to me.

"Nothing." I pulled a piece of thread from Ernest's dull green bedspread with my free hand. "Just leaving."

"So do it," she said, her hands on her hips, a teapot with no spout.

"Is that a Vermeer?" I asked, pointing to a small painting in a deep gold frame of a girl in a red hat. The light on her face looked warm and real. Her mouth was open, like she was about to speak.

"You know Vermeer?" Ernest said, trying to sit up.

"Let's go, Iris," Hannah said, and she looked hard at me as if to say, *It's mine.*

To Ernest she said, "She can bore you with questions another time."

While the nurse hooked up another bag of fluids to Ernest's drip, my mother bent close to his face.

"If there's anything I can do for you," she said, more business-like than kind, "just let me know."

Ernest let his eyes roll back in his head. He dropped my hand as he started to cough, a wet thundercloud that rumbled through his body and left him weak and sweating on the bed. He hacked away until the noise drove Hannah out, and she drove me from the room.

"As if she had any bargaining power left," he told me later. "As if your mother had anything anymore that I wanted."

Six

Hannah and Lowell marked out their territory like tomcats, and Ernest's house soon stank of perfume and vodka and ashtray and, under that, something foul like rotten meat. I think it was their livers. The two of them drank all day, which was nothing new. You could always hear where they were in a house by the clink of ice cubes in glasses. Hannah's high heels left flinty marks on the floorboards and four-inch spike holes in the garden. She measured out her day in tightly sealed boxes: two minutes for snapping through a magazine, two for a cigarette, two for checking in on Ernest—when she worried she hadn't been faking concern well enough—whispering with Lowell, or barking at the nurses, or at me. It was clear she was just killing time, waiting for the Grim Reaper to arrive, looking at her watch like he was late and she was paying him by the hour. She bounced from wall to wall, over and over, like a fly mapping a room.

Lowell prowled the perimeters of things, noticing himself in every reflective surface. He passed the time picking up ornaments and looking underneath them, like a secret service agent checking for bugs. It struck me that the way he moved was precise and considered because the one person really fully watching him do anything was himself. Now and then, he posed at a fireplace or a window and turned his face so that the light hit him just right—screen idol, male model, action man. I would never accuse my stepfather of being the sharpest tool in the box, but he has a pretty good instinct for flattering lighting.

Ernest made a big effort to be out of bed. The nurses helped him downstairs and wheeled him out into the sheltered courtyard, tethered to his oxygen, the ends of his nose and fingers slowly turning grayish blue. He sat with us, pale and sweating, swaddled in blankets, and looked out over the bright lawn while we were eating lunch. Hannah took in his waxy, unshaven face and his labored, bubbly breathing and let her fork drop into her salad—disgust disguised as fullness, like she'd ever needed an excuse not to eat. I could see the scowl behind her sunglasses as she lit another cigarette.

She'd already been to see Jane in the kitchen and handed over her list of sugar-free, low-carb, low-calorie, no-gluten, no-dairy, organic, California-style, fresh-only demands. Hannah will only smoke her way through the very best ingredients. Jane was overweight, with marbled arms and legs and sensible shoes and a chin that flowed straight into her neck. You could tell she was more suet than tofu. She scanned my mother's recipes with her shiny raisin eyes.

"You won't get almond milk here," she said.

"So get it delivered."

Hannah was about three feet taller than Jane in her heels. They didn't look like the same species.

"He only eats soup."

"Well, his guests don't. And don't screw up, or I'll make sure he fires you."

At the lunch table, Ernest's chin slumped low against his chest, eyes closed. The breeze whipped his hair about in little tufts like cotton candy. I could see Jane and the nurses watching us from the kitchen window.

Hannah looked at Lowell. "I don't trust any of those women. Gold-diggers, I'm telling you."

"Well, you would know," I said as she flicked ash into her lamb's lettuce.

"This is different."

"In what way?"

Hannah looked over at Ernest. "We're family."

I laughed. "Since when?"

"Since I said so, Iris," she said, standing up before the rest of us had finished. "Since we came here to get what we deserve."

She went inside to get herself another drink. Lowell left the table too. That day he was on a pretty short leash. Once they were both gone, Ernest opened his eyes and winked at me. At least I think he did.

"I thought you were asleep," I said.

He shook his head. "Resting. Listening."

He pulled the blankets tighter around him even though the sun was out, and it was pretty warm.

"It's pretty much your own fault," I said.

"What is?"

"I don't know. All of it."

He closed his eyes again. "I see."

"Have you ever seen *The Royal Tenenbaums*?" I asked him.

"Is it a painting?"

"No, a movie."

"About what?"

"About a group of grown-up child prodigies who get together because their dad is dying."

"And you like it?" he asked me.

I nodded. "Family *isn't a word. It's a sentence.*"

I looked out across the fields toward the black shadows of the mountains.

"It's good to see you, Iris."

"Yeah, well, you could have seen me sooner if you had ever invited me," I said, and it sounded more spiteful than I meant.

I knew Ernest was looking at me, but I didn't take my eyes off the view. "You and I need to find more reasons to be alone together," he said.

"We do? Why?"

"We have a lot to talk about."

"Like what?"

"There are some things I'd like you to know," he said. "Things about me. About you and me."

There were tubes running into the back of his hand, stuck down with tape. His veins looked risen and solid, like twigs.

"Not to be rude or anything," I told him, and we both knew I meant the exact opposite, "but isn't all this a bit late?"

"I couldn't have put it better myself," he said.

"So what's the point, then?" I said.

Ernest sighed. He sagged slowly, the way an inflatable does when the party's over and the air's leaking out.

"We can fight if you like," he said. "We can do all of that. It's your choice. But I want you to know, we might not have time to make up."

Jane came outside to clear the plates. Her cheeks were the color of raspberries. The bony points of her body, her knuckles and elbows and wrists, were lost in her flesh, like someone inside a duvet.

"How are you, Mr. Jones?"

"Still alive," he said drily. "Always a bonus."

We could hear Hannah inside the house, raising her voice over something.

"Are my guests being difficult?"

She looked straight at him. "I don't know who she thinks she is."

"The lady of the house," Ernest told her. "My wife."

"You're still married?" I said. "You've got to be kidding."

Ernest nodded. "Twenty-one years this November."

Jane's jowls shook like a basset hound's. "Is there anything else I can get for you?"

"A bottle of the widow," he said, "and four glasses."

"Should you be drinking, sir?"

"No."

Jane frowned.

"We're celebrating," he said. "I'll just taste it." He put a hand on her arm. "And thank you, Jane, for asking."

A short time later, she carried the loaded tray back across the grass, her apron caught in her waistband, her thighs like bolster cushions in her jeans. It was nice, the way she spoke to Ernest, like it was her job, but she cared about him anyway. I liked her for that, even if I didn't like him all that much.

"What are we celebrating?" I said. "Your long and happy marriage?"

Here I was, thousands of miles away from home, worried about Thurston, trapped in the wrong place, a pawn in some old war between Ernest and my mother.

It wasn't a champagne moment for me.

He leaned back in his chair, blinked up at the sky, and tried his hardest to breathe.

"I'm not sure yet," he said. "We'll have to wait and see."

Hannah and Lowell emerged from inside the house, trailing Jane and the bottle like iron filings behind a magnet. My mother was at the isn't-everything-great stage of drunk. She arranged herself in her chair and sighed loudly.

"Champagne," she said. "How marvelous."

Ernest looked at Lowell and pointed at the tray. "Do the honors, would you?"

Lowell popped the cork, and Hannah showed more teeth. I could see her eyeing the bottle, trying to calculate how much was left.

"A toast," Ernest said, raising his glass. "To us."

My mother's laugh was quick and shrill and high. "I'll drink to that," she said, as if there were things in the world she wouldn't drink to.

"Hear, hear," said Lowell.

"To family," Ernest said, looking only at me. "Whatever that might mean."

Seven

When they could afford it, Thurston and Uncle Mac used to buy lapsed storage units and sift through things once precious enough to keep safe and then abandoned. He said it was like buying into whole lives. You pieced together what you knew about somebody from the things they'd done their best to save. Vivien Maier's photographs were found that way, her life's work bought in job lots at auction after she died. Thurston spread out everything he bought like a map and then photographed it, and each photo had the name of the person who'd owned it. Leonard D. Theil. Marsha Louise Hunter. Margot Florian Jones.

Apparently, I reminded Ernest of his sister, Margot.

Sometimes, when the pain got really bad and he went to town on the morphine, he thought I was Margot, come to visit. He talked to her instead of talking to me, and I pieced her together from the things Ernest said, like one of Thurston's photos. It seemed too cruel to set him straight. And in some ways it took the pressure off having to be myself. I could just sit back and listen.

Hannah didn't like him talking to me. She made up chores for me to do, and reasons to ride into town on my bike. She said I should get outside more, like she cared about my vitamin D levels, and not just that I was spending too much time with Ernest.

Whenever I could, though, I climbed the stairs to his room and let him talk. If Ernest said, "How are you, Margot?" I said I was fine. If he said, "Do you remember the time when?" I said, "No, tell me again."

He talked about this grassy bank at the foot of the garden. When he was a boy, the gardener told him it was a burial mound for an elephant. The circus had come to town in 1832, and the elephant had caught the flu and died.

"You can't do much with a dead elephant," the gardener had said, "except bury it."

Ernest wanted to dig down and find the elephant's skeleton the way an archaeologist unearths a dinosaur. He wanted to dust at its bones with toothpicks and paintbrushes, but he wasn't allowed. The gardener said they weren't to disturb the dead, and Margot said, "Quite right. Leave them where they damn well are. They've had their turn."

"You said the elephant would come and haunt me as punishment for wanting to open up its grave," Ernest told me. "You warned me to listen for its footsteps at midnight and then you paced the corridor outside my room banging that drum until I wet myself in terror and you skidded off to bed."

I smiled. "Sorry," I said.

Ernest waved his hands at me. "Don't be. You were always worth more than the trouble you caused. I've missed you, Margot. It's been far too long."

Ernest reminded me of an elephant. The skin around his eyes was thick and dark and wrinkled, like an elephant's eye. And there were so many things he seemed to never forget. Once he got started, I think he carried on talking even when he was the only one left in the room, like a juggernaut too big and slow to turn around in a hurry. He was telling his life from start to finish, and it didn't seem to matter if anyone could hear him or not. Sometimes I listened from out in the hall because I didn't want to go in and disturb him. I didn't want to interrupt his flow.

I learned that Margot got sent away to school but Ernest stayed home because of a weak chest and allergies and something else his mom had called an indoor disposition and his dad had called a damn shame. He had tutors for math and science. His dad taught him French and some military history, and his mom taught him everything she knew about her favorite artists. The family owned a handful of valuable paintings.

When he wasn't studying, Ernest was performing. "I was a good mimic," he said. "I used to entertain them with my impressions of famous film stars and politicians. I had a talent for it."

I listened to Ernest's ramblings, and I thought this was where Thurston should be, listening with me, sitting with his knees up and his back against the wall. He'd have loved it. They would have been instant, good friends. I have no doubt about that.

Ernest said his parents thought it was Margot who should be sitting quietly when she was at home, but Margot liked to ride and climb and swim and row and shoot.

"Can you still serve a ball straight onto a coin eight times out of ten?" he asked me when he was asking her. "Can you still scale a tree like a primate?"

He said she was proud of her mud-streaked shins and filthy clothes and uncombed hair. It was Margot who caught a fish with her bare hands and bashed its brains out on the stones of the shrunken riverbed. Ernest could only watch. She brought it home, gutted it with her penknife and cooked it over an open fire. Her parents said that was no way for a young woman to behave.

"Thank God," said Margot, pulling fish bones out of her teeth, wiping her mouth on her sleeve. "I have no intention of ever behaving like one."

She called Ernest a mama's boy, and Ernest was so struck by the idea that he cried and proved her right. But he liked to think he protected Margot, in his way, from the sharpened arrows of their expectations, the bullets of their many disappointments. By being their constant companion, the child they could control, he took their attention away from his tomboy sister.

"Stand up straight," they snapped at him when Margot slouched past.

"Your hair is a disgrace," they said, looking the other way as Margot pulled herself backward through the box hedge and cut across the square, flat lawn, her own hair stuck with twigs and dressed with feathers.

Ernest half smiled at me in the hazy, shut-curtained gloom of his room. "I was always in trouble because of you, Margot," he said.

"One spike or two?" she'd say, and if he asked why, she'd tell him, "Because you're such a goddamn martyr. Live a little, for God's sake. Stop minding so much what people think."

Thurston would have liked Margot too. He'd have approved of the way she was different from the rest of her family. He always said the best people stick out like sore thumbs, that the black sheep are the ones to watch.

"Look at you," he said. "You're nothing like who you should be."

"And you?" I asked him. "What is your family like?"

"Gun-toting, stranger-bashing, rage-twisted, tightfisted creationists," Thurston said. "I haven't spoken to them in years. I had myself emancipated in a court of law. I can't see how we're even related."

Neither of us spoke for a minute and then he said, "Please don't ask me about them again."

Ernest told me that at eighteen, Margot eloped with a taxi driver and lost a small fortune at a casino in the South of France. A month later, she ran off to New York with a camera salesman. Her parents washed their hands of her after her third affair—with an ex–airline pilot—and a bit of light smuggling. They paid off the judge and then they cut Margot off without a penny, which was what she'd wanted all along. She used to tell Ernest that being born into money had made them all worthless and unmotivated.

"Look at you," she said, teasing. "They may as well have pulled out your spine."

Ernest said she went to London, trained as a nurse, and joined a team of doctors working in conflict zones and refugee camps, in the paths of epidemics and earthquakes and hurricanes. She never once visited home. She was done with it. She sent Ernest postcards from all the far-flung, war-torn, disease-ridden, beautiful places she wound up.

So very different, she would write, *from the home life of our own dear Queen.*

If his parents got to them first, her cards ended up in pieces in the trash and Ernest had to put them together like a puzzle. He marked each place in his atlas with an X, so he could see at a glance where his sister was, and how far from them she had gone.

"Don't hang around, little brother," she told him. "Get out while you can. Times are changing. There's a whole world out there. Honestly, I do things that would turn your hair gray overnight, and nobody bats an eyelid."

But all Ernest wanted to think about was art.

"What good is the real," he asked me once, "when there are so many more beautiful versions of it to distract you?"

He stayed behind with his books and his parents. When his dad died of a heart attack at sixty, Ernest took over the family collection. He sent works to galleries and institutions on loan. He bought when the price was low and sold at a profit. He had a feel for it. He and his mom sat for hours at the feet of Rossettis and O'Keeffes, of Pollocks and Rembrandts and Gentileschis, of Kahlos and Hockneys and Rothkos. She broke their silences with updates on the absent. "Margot would hate this," or, "I want you to sell the little Gauguin," or, "Your father would have closed this deal by now."

He disappeared into his work, all alone in that house, and it suited him.

"You were right, Margot," he told me. "There was a whole world out there, and I avoided it like the plague."

"You did what you wanted," I said. "That's OK, isn't it?"

He smiled. "But just think of all the life I missed while I was living my own."

Margot died in a house fire in Nairobi when she was twenty-nine. She would have been almost sixty by now. Their mom died on a flight from Colombia to New York. The plane ran out of fuel and crashed into a hillside on Long Island's North Shore. That night at home there was a storm. Ernest had no electricity for three days because the winds had wrecked the power lines. Otherwise, he might have known sooner. He thought the trees were going to come crashing through his bedroom window. He was awake all night, waiting for it to happen. He didn't know yet that he was the only one left.

I don't think Ernest believed his family was together in some form or another in the afterlife, waiting for him. He didn't expect to see them again anytime soon.

"I miss Margot," he said when he remembered I was Iris and she was gone. "She was my best friend."

In spite of everything, I felt bad for him. "I've lost one of those," I told him.

"It hurts, doesn't it?" he said.

"It does," I said. "Yes."

"Her name?"

"Who?"

"Your friend."

"Oh, his name. He's a he. Thurston. Thurston Shaw."

"Great name."

"Great person."

"Tell me about this Thurston," he said. "What does he do? Why do you like him?"

"He's an artist, I suppose. Not just nine to five, not for money or anything. He just sort of lives it."

"Sounds reckless."

"He's brave," I said. "And smart, and colorful, and funny."

Ernest smiled. "And how did you lose him?"

I told him I hadn't seen Thurston since a week before we left the States. I said he had no idea where I was, and I had no way of finding him, either.

"We had a falling-out," I said. "I don't think he was talking to me."

He smiled again. "What did you do?"

I felt like crying. That doesn't happen often, to me. "I hurt his feelings," I told him. "I said some things I shouldn't. And then I got dragged here, so I lost him. He's a needle in a haystack."

Ernest nodded. "The world is a very big place when you're looking for someone."

I felt the truth of what he said, heavy in the pit of my stomach.

"I miss him," I said. "And I don't know what I'm supposed to do next."

"Get on with the business of living," Ernest told me. "You don't have any other choice."

Eight

The second time I met Thurston, I was burning leaves in an empty swimming pool on an abandoned lot over by Long Beach, repossession central. The pool liner was this bright grimy turquoise, and the leaves that had fallen into it were copper and chestnut and desert red. I was happy. I remember that. I looked up through the thick, sweet smoke, and he was standing on the edge, looking down at me. I recognized him immediately, the boy from the subway, still tall, still pale, still skinny. Suddenly there was a point to things, a reason for them. That's what it felt like, seeing him again.

"Hey," he said. "It's you," and he smiled. "Do you remember me? From the subway?"

I nodded. "The boy with the messages."

"Did you start the fire on Willow and Melrose," he said, "in the bakery?"

"No," I said.

He dropped his head to one side, crinkled up his eyes. "Are you sure?"

"I don't do buildings," I said. "Not working ones. Not like that."

"But swimming pools are OK."

I shrugged. "I'm just tidying up."

He looked around at the weed-choked yard, at the broken lawn chairs and left-behind toys and smashed-up deck. "That's one way of putting it."

He jumped in, one hand on the side, landing light on his feet in the dry deep end.

The leaves spat and settled around him, and he put his hand out over the flames to shake mine.

"Thurston," he said.

"Iris."

"How old are you?" he asked.

"Almost fourteen," I said. "You?"

He smiled. "Almost seventeen."

79

He picked up an armful of leaves and dumped them on the heap, but before he did it, he asked me if it was OK. "May I?" he said. I liked that.

I watched the fire for a quiet, crackling minute.

"Sure. Go ahead."

Leaves have this tang when they're burning, like nuked fruit juice. I can't think of a better way to put it than that.

"You need a mark," he said.

"What?"

"A sign or something."

"Why?"

"To say which fires are yours. Show where you've been. So I know."

"So you know? Why do you want to know?"

He shrugged. "I wouldn't want to wait so long next time, to see you."

He got these paint cans out of his jacket and started spraying the wall of the pool. His back was half to me and I couldn't see what he was doing, but it was over pretty quick and when he stepped back, there was an eye: sharp black pupil, clean white ball, swirling bright circle of color.

"Iris," he said. "That's you," and then he jumped up out of

the pool like there was still water in it to lift him. I didn't want him to go.

"Use it if you want," he said. "See you around."

Back home I practiced drawing it the way he did, until I got it right. After that, I started leaving little eyes in all sorts of places: along my ride to school, outside our apartment, on the boarded-up windows of the emptied houses, their lightless rooms dark against the sky like missing teeth. It got to be a habit. It got so I couldn't stop. When I saw that eye up against a door or an illegal ad or a stretch of ground, I knew I was somewhere and that Thurston was somewhere too, noticing me.

Nobody really noticed me at Ernest's. It wasn't about me, and that was fine. There was this tug-of-war going on—the nurses on one side doing what they could to keep him comfortable and alive, Hannah and Lowell on the other side willing him to die, giving it all they'd got. I guess I slipped through a gap somewhere in the middle, because it was the quietest place to be. I kept thinking that if I could just tune in to the right frequency, I'd hear the sound of all that struggle, the way a dog hears things streets away that don't even register with the human ear.

And then after two or three days of doing his best to hope for the worst, Lowell decided it was time to go back to the apartment in London, or maybe my mother decided for him; it's always hard to tell. He was happy enough to do it. He was up for a role in a daytime soap, so he needed to get back and get to grips with his Yorkshire accent. I had no idea he was leaving until I saw him with his suitcase in the hall. He didn't even stop walking. He waved at me over his shoulder. He couldn't get out of there fast enough.

"You're going?" I said.

"I've got a job. An audition. They asked for me."

I followed him out to the car. "Since when?"

Lowell threw his suitcase down on the backseat and slammed the door. He was already somewhere else. In his head, he'd finished filming, been taken out for lunch and offered a spin-off series of his own. That's how his mind works. The only thing that's ever mattered to Lowell is his big break, and he's kind of heroic, I suppose, for always charging after it, for believing without fail that it's just around the corner. He could take or leave most of the real world, but he'd go to the ends of the earth for a sniff of fame. I guess that's how we ended up in LA in the first place, chasing Lowell's disappearing dream. It's an addiction of sorts, like Hannah's credit card problem, or my thing with fire. You'd have thought we'd all understand one another better by now.

"I'd say you're here to the bitter end, kiddo," he said, and he winked because he really couldn't have cared less, and got in the car. My mother came outside and stood behind me as Lowell gunned it up the drive and onto the road.

"Right," she said, clapping her hands together, turning back toward the house. "Let's get to work."

"What are we doing?" I asked her.

"Do you remember that place we rented in San Diego?" she said.

"Yeah."

"Do you remember how the landlord had a list of every single damn thing in that apartment so that when somebody broke the lightshade and the lounge chairs, he kept all the money from our deposit?"

Hannah and Lowell threw one hell of a party in that place when he got a speaking part in a movie (third cop—he ended up on the cutting-room floor). The lightshade broke because four half-dressed people were swinging on it. The lounge chairs got thrown into the pool. I was eight or nine. Three different men came into my room that night and tried to pee in the corner.

"I remember," I said.

"Well, we're going to make a list like that," Hannah said.

"Of what?"

"Of everything in this house. So we know what's coming to us when he dies."

"Seriously?"

"Room by room," she said. "If anything goes missing, I want to be able to tell."

"Does Ernest know?" I asked.

Hannah looked at me like I hadn't been listening. "Of course he doesn't know. And there's no need to tell him. He's unconscious most of the time. He doesn't even know what day it is."

"I think he does."

I'd started to think that Ernest was overdoing it a bit when Hannah was around. Not faking it exactly, but he got drowsier when she walked into the room. He sagged and drooled and aged. He was hiding from her behind the thing she was so busy seeing, which was how little time he had left.

"He's on his way out," she said. "He's half gone already."

"Nice," I told her. "Really softhearted."

"This is insurance," she said. "I'm thinking ahead. I'm protecting our assets. I'm trying to do the right thing."

To be clear, my mother has never tried to do the right thing. In fact, she wouldn't know the right thing if it hit her square in the face. But she's a survivor, I guess. She knows how to keep her head above water, if nothing else.

She handed me a notebook and a pen.

"Start in the dining room," she said. "I know for a fact there's Baccarat crystal in there, and box loads of eighteenth-century silver. Just count it and write it down. That's a new car at least, in one side table. You have no idea how wealthy Ernest is. And we haven't even started on the art."

"You're enjoying yourself, aren't you," I said.

"Don't take this the wrong way," she said with a straight face, like there was any other way to take it, "but it's the answer to all our problems. This is a fresh start for us. Ernest couldn't be doing this at a better time."

I walked away from her.

"Oh, and Iris," she said, her chin stuck out in fight mode, her teeth pressed so tight together I could see the line of her jaw. Hannah has this thing about a double chin, like it's an offense worse than murder to ever get one. The tendons in her neck stand up under her skin like witch's fingers, like a handful of sticks.

"What?"

"If you find matches, or a lighter, and you put them to any-thing, *anything* in this house, I swear to God I'll—"

"You'll what?" I said.

"I'll *kill* you."

It was her fault. She started it.

I pictured her collapsed and wailing by a heap of burning treasure, and I couldn't stop smiling.

"What's so funny?" she asked me.

"Now you're just putting ideas into my head," I said.

Nine

Back home, before we left everything behind, Hannah's closet was filled to bursting with all her best things: her skirts and handbags, her elaborate, wire-boned underwear, and all of her spike-heeled, angry-looking shoes. More than half her debts probably occupied the shelves and hangers in that thing, walk-in proof of her compulsive shopping habit, her addiction to plastic, serotonin, and sky-high rates of interest. She tended that closet like you would a garden. She lavished more attention on those few square feet than she'd ever mustered up for me.

What can I say? It went up in flames like it was born to, like it had only ever wanted to burn.

It wasn't spite. I didn't plan it. It was the first time I

lit a fire because things got beyond my control. I don't remember having any say in the matter. I don't recall there being a choice.

She and Lowell were throwing a lunch party for some hotshot media couple, a casting director and an agent, I think, some supposedly irresistible combination of power. They'd been planning it for months, like it might actually amount to something. Lowell couldn't get enough of grabbing me by the arm and telling me in a hushed kind of shout how important this was, how make-or-break, careerwise. And I got it. I'm not all bad. Awkwardness aside, I was willing to try.

This couple had brought their Neanderthal teenage son, Jesse, with them, so it was my job to look after him. When they showed up, everyone got a drink and Jesse was tall and broad and charm and politeness and straight teeth. He said "yes, sir" and "no, ma'am" like some perfect, cherry-pie-eating, football-playing, all-American dreamboat. Hannah was quite taken with him. I could see that. She has a better smile for the attractive ones, however old or young they might be. She looks up at them so you can see the low whites of her eyes.

Everyone was getting along fine in a fake kind of way, and after a while, Jesse asked to see my room.

"Good idea," said Hannah, biting into the surface of her ice-cold vodka. "You youngsters go ahead and get acquainted."

On the way up the stairs, I told him there wasn't much to look at, and Jesse pulled a fat joint out of his pocket and smiled.

He said, "I'm sure we'll stay entertained."

We smoked the joint and my head felt heavy on my neck and numb like I'd stuffed it with wet cotton balls. I wanted to be out in the open air with Thurston, not shut in with this plastic-perfect jock. I took Jesse's box of matches and held on to it, as if it were the guardrail and we were two hundred stories up. I had a kind of shadow on me that I couldn't shake off. He looked at me and laughed and laughed.

It turned out we had very different ideas of what entertainment meant. After ten minutes, he had me pinned under him on my single bed. His breath was sour and hot in my face, and his eyes were glazed over, like he didn't even see me anymore. He tore my T-shirt. He hurt my arms.

"Get off me," I said, but he didn't.

"Don't touch me," I said, but he did.

I could see my shut door from where I was lying. I shouted. I called "HANNAH" and "HELP ME" and "SOMEONE PLEASE," and I could hear them downstairs, I could hear their low stupid jazz and their giddy, getting-to-know-you laughter, so how come they couldn't hear me? When Jesse started undoing his fly, I dug my nails into his face hard and pulled, got out from under him, and ran.

I quickly locked myself in Hannah and Lowell's bedroom. I heard Jesse moaning and cursing and calling me a frigid little bitch. The fire started in me then. I felt it ignite. My parents were downstairs pinning their hopes, networking like crazy, playing host like the rest of their lives depended on it, and I knew they'd already failed, because of me. That bastard Jesse would go in bleeding and make up some story, and the whole thing would be over before it had really begun. They hadn't even served the food yet.

I went into Hannah's closet to hide. I listened. It was dark and quiet, and my heart was pounding in my ears like bass from a speaker. Jesse must have gone down around then, because I heard a scream and raised voices, and Hannah's footsteps on the stairs.

I still had Jesse's matchbox. I shook it and the matches ratcheted up against one end and then the other. I pushed it a little way open and touched them where they were sleeping, then I tipped them into the palm of my hand and counted them one by one. There were twenty. Ask anyone who's interested, twenty matches is a *find*, twenty fires if you don't waste any and you pay attention to what you're doing.

Hannah was storming across the top floor, swearing and slamming things, looking for me. She tried the door of her bedroom. I heard the handle rattle.

"Get out here, Iris," she said. "Get out here and explain yourself."

I stayed where I was.

"He touched me," I said.

"He *what*?"

"He hurt me," I said, and I expected her to be shocked, to feel bad for me, or at the very least to get it, but she didn't.

"Don't be ridiculous," she said, her voice slicing through the bedroom door and the door of the closet. "Come out right now and say sorry."

I swear, my own rage might have eaten me up just like fire right then if I hadn't had hold of those matches. I held on to that first one a little while before I struck it. I didn't turn the light on. I folded myself up in the dark and the quiet, bringing my breath back down to normal, feeling the weight of the match hardly there in my hand, rubbing the tip with my thumb.

When I brought it down on the side of the box, it sparked fast, orange-white, and then it flamed up bright and lit my skin a deep golden yellow in the gloom. I held on to it until the spent end glowed and then dimmed, black and withered and done. One delicate curl of smoke furled upward like an opening fern when I dropped it.

"Are you listening to me, Iris?" she said.

"No," I yelled at her, my mouth pressed up against the door.

I did it again. The smell of the second match was like hot sun and brimstone and dust and autumn leaf. There was a space at the base of the flame, a little wavering hollow, and I couldn't take my eyes off of it. It was that silence and emptiness I craved, the absence at the heart of it. I wanted to climb right in. Nobody would think to bother me in there.

My mother didn't let up. She told me I was selfish and ungrateful and unhinged. The longer I stayed quiet, the more toxic she got. She said a lot of things through that door, but I didn't satisfy her with an answer. I no longer felt the need to reply.

I struck seven or eight matches and watched them burn out before I held one to the net hem of her favorite dress. It went up like paper, and in less than half a minute, Hannah's entire rack of clothes was raging. The paint on the closet wall started to blister.

The harder it burned, the calmer I felt, the quieter it was in my head. I came out slowly. I shut the closet door and watched smoke pumping itself through all the cracks and spaces it could find, in a great rush to get out into the room. The flames started coming with it, feasting on my mother's possessions, devouring her closet from the inside out.

"Iris?" she screamed, banging on the bedroom door with her fists. "What's going on?"

I pulled the door open and walked straight past her like she wasn't there. The smoke rolled out of the room. The glass in her hand fell and bounced against the baseboard, trailing droplets of vodka like tears. She said "SHIT" and "WHAT THE—?" and "OH MY GOD, IRIS, JESUS CHRIST" and then Lowell came running. The two of them filled jugs and bowls with tap water and flung them at the fire. They drowned towels and blankets in the shower and dragged them down the hall to throw on to the flames. They were all activity and repetition, like a panicked hive. I didn't help. I didn't want to put my fire out. I wanted it to burn and burn.

When it was done, they took turns wailing and yelling until I stopped hearing them, until there was no air left in the room to carry the sound.

At some point, the power couple took their darling boy home. They saw themselves out before anyone could stop them. Jesse got away with it. Hannah was too busy crying in the wreckage of her stupid outfits, her Louboutins and her Ungaro and her Donna Fucking Karan.

"You might have killed us all," she said, fists full of ruined fabric.

Lowell had his head in his hands. He'd already turned that almost-lunch into the mythic, one clear chance of his acting career. He'd already decided it would be my fault now if he didn't make it.

He asked me what the hell I was thinking. I picked at a hole in my shorts, and I didn't bother to tell him that the beauty of it was that I hadn't been thinking at all. That's the thing about a good fire. It empties your head completely. It razes everything to the ground so there's nothing left. It's the very definition of calm.

I took in the stench and the smoke and the soaked carpet and the ruined, irreplaceable clothes and the great smoldering wound of a closet, and I couldn't shake the feeling that it was worth it. I knew I would have done it all again.

That night, instead of sleeping, I thought about what else I might like to burn to the ground. I thought about Jesse, trapped in a building, with all the exits blocked, eaten alive by flames. I wished for an inferno wherever he was harder than I'd wished for anything else in my simmering, sad little life.

And early the next morning, while Hannah and Lowell were still sleeping it off downstairs, I went into their damp and blackened room with my old paint set, and I painted an eye on the window, the pupil small and black, the eyeball white, and the iris as close as I could get it to the color of fire, like someone staring into a flame. When I left the house to look for Thurston, it watched me. It followed me all the way down the street.

And it didn't blink.

Ten

The first night Hannah and I were alone in Ernest's house, the day Lowell left, I got called into Ernest's room very late. Lisa the night nurse crept in to get me.

"Who's that?" I said, sitting up in the dark.

"He's asking for you, Iris."

In his room, Ernest held on to my hand like he'd fallen into quicksand and I was the one pulling him out. He said there were things he hadn't explained yet. He said he needed to unburden himself, and I thought, *Oh, here we go. He's going to get it all off his chest and dump it on mine.*

"Do you have to?" I said, and he seemed to think about it. I gave him some credit for that.

But then I stayed quiet. I thought it was the smart thing to do. I tried to make a list in my head of places I'd rather be. 1. With Thurston. 2. The airport. 3. The Grand Canyon. 4. The middle of the ocean. 5. Mars.

There were tulips from the garden in a vase by Ernest's bed. There was a time centuries ago when tulips were worth more than their weight in gold, when a man would trade one single bulb for his whole house and all of its contents, would risk his life and liberty just to own it. It's nuts when you think about it, how easily we lose our minds over stuff, how quickly money eats up the world, just like fire.

I thought about fire eating up Ernest's house, the heavy dark furniture and the curtains and the paintings and the dust. I thought about a bright flame wiping it clean and then I realized he was talking to me.

"It's all yours," he was saying. "All of it. It's all for you."

"Are we talking about money?" I said. "Because I'm not interested in money. It's not why I came. I keep telling everyone that."

"Why did you come?" Ernest asked, and I told him the truth.

"My mother made me. I didn't have a choice."

Ernest coughed, and his lungs rattled. "Not money—paintings.

And the house, of course. I'd like you to have the paintings and the house."

"Ernest," I said, but he didn't hear me.

"No death duties," he said, "no stealth taxes. Everything is in a trust for when you're eighteen. I've been looking after it."

"Hannah wants your money," I said. "Not me."

He looked at me then like he was seeing me for the first time, like he hadn't really looked at me before.

"I've never loved anybody the way I loved you," he said, and it shocked me, the way he just came out with it. It made me want to curl up in a tight ball. It made me want to hide. My face was hot like an ember.

"Yeah, right," I said.

He looked angry and frail. "I haven't done it well. I've failed, and it's been an exhausting, vicious, lonely, overwhelming thing."

I didn't want to feel sorry for him, but I did, and it made me furious. "I can't do this," I said, and I started to leave.

"Do you remember anything," he said, "about me?"

"What is there to remember?"

"You've got me all wrong, Iris."

"No, Ernest, I haven't got you at all."

It was the middle of the night, for God's sake. I was tired and all I wanted to do was be somewhere else. I couldn't deal with this. I hadn't asked for any of it.

"I just want you to know the truth. I just need you to listen."

"OK," I said, but I stayed where I was, by the door, waiting. "So tell me about you and my mom. Why were you ever together? How the hell did that happen in the first place?"

Eleven

Ernest tripped on a paving stone. He fell like a tree right in front of my mother on an Oxford side street and cut his face on something sharp. He said there was a lot of blood. Hannah helped him to sit up with his back against the window of an antique shop, his legs out in front of him on the pavement.

"That surprises me," I said. "The Hannah Baxter I know and love would have walked straight past you."

Ernest's eyes were glazed and exhausted. "Perhaps she hadn't turned into her yet."

He said it took him a minute to remember the rumpled suit trousers and the scuffed shoes he was looking at were his. There was a fine set of wineglasses in the shop window behind him, fanciful and delicate, with slender glass stems. They might have been dancing around his head like fairies, like stars in a cartoon. He turned to see what she was looking at, the blood still welling from the bridge of his nose.

"Handmade," he said through his darkening handkerchief, "1920s. Probably French."

Hannah smiled. "I'm sure I would drop one."

"Pretty pricey. Couple hundred a pop."

"I could live on that for a month," she said.

My mother's eyes were the color of sand and envelopes. Ernest said she was bundled up against the cold, a scarf over her mouth and chin, a hat pulled down low, an oversized coat. He couldn't see anything of her at first but her brown-paper eyes and her thin, pale hands.

I saw some photos a while ago, extreme close-ups of the human eye. They were like the surfaces of planets, those pictures, like whole worlds and the skin of rope and the mouths of volcanoes. I know the color of my mother's eyes. They must have looked like deserts, sand dunes caving in on themselves in ceaseless winds. Ernest said he would have been happy to wander in them forever. I said her eyes were about as hospitable as a desert too, and he wouldn't have wandered happily for long without water, or a camel, or someone to save him.

"She wasn't always like that," he told me, and I said, "Whatever."

When the ambulance arrived, Ernest was embarrassed. He didn't want any fuss. He wanted to know who'd called for one, but the paramedics wouldn't say. He felt horribly visible. He knew people were watching from behind their curtains.

"Would *you* take me home?" he asked her.

"I can't." Hannah shook her head. He saw that her coat was stained and worn thin at the elbows. Her mouth was as pale as her skin. "I don't have a car."

"You could drive mine." He patted his bruised face. It was beginning to swell. "I'm having trouble seeing past my own nose."

He didn't tell her that home was almost two hours away. He wasn't ready for her to say no. One of the paramedics asked Hannah if she was responsible for him and so Ernest answered for her. He said that she was.

"It was my doing," he told me, "all of it."

They walked slowly to his 1946 Bentley, iron gray, sleek as a cat. She was taller than him, and thin as a rake. When he put his hand on her back to show her the way, he could feel the hard knuckles of her spine. He said Hannah raised her eyebrows at the car. She ran her fingers along its flanks like it was a living thing. Before she tried to start the engine, she took off her hat. Her long dark hair filled the car with its scent and made him dizzy. There were holes in her clothes, some badly mended, some not. She wore no makeup. She gripped the steering wheel until the bones in her hands showed white.

"That doesn't sound like her at all," I said.

"She was different then," he told me. "She had nothing to lose."

Ernest asked Hannah to tell him something about herself. She said there was nothing to tell.

"Where do you live?" he said.

"Other people's sofas."

"What do you do?" he said, and she shrugged instead of answering. The silence wasn't something she felt obliged to fill.

She crossed and uncrossed her long legs. Ernest said he tried his best not to look at them. He'd been to the Ashmolean Museum to see the world's largest collection of Raphael drawings. He'd studied them carefully, but he'd been unable to reach his usual hypnotic state. Other people kept breaking his concentration. Students and couples and pensioners, having a day out, lost in conversation, just glancing at the art. Now here he was in a trance, in his own car, with this lean girl and her long limbs, fluid as a Boldini portrait, and her eyes on him while he waited for her to start the car.

Hannah wound down her window and let in the winter air. The wind was blowing in from the Arctic, the weather people had said. It had passed through Svalbard and Norway and the Faroe Islands on its way to them in their dot on the landscape—that parking space. That was all Ernest could think about, that and her legs and her hair.

She turned the key in the ignition. "Where to?"

"It's a long way," he confessed. "Just under a hundred miles."

Hannah smiled. "Will you buy me lunch?" she said, and he nodded.

"If you like."

"I don't have anywhere else to be."

They stopped at a pub, and she ate like she hadn't eaten in a while, like she wasn't sure where her next meal was coming from. She was starving, he realized. And after she'd eaten, he drove so she could sleep, and he tried to keep his eyes on the road.

At the house, he showed her around. He pulled out all the stops: his dad's vintage cars, his art collection. My mother took it all in.

"This has got to be worth *millions*," she cooed, putting her

104

perfect upturned nose against the cold skin of a Picasso Blue Nude.

She spent the night in one of the guest rooms. It hadn't been slept in for years. They uncovered the antique rosewood furniture, the bed and chest and dressing table. The air swam with dust that gathered in the space around them like plankton around whales. Ernest had a sneezing fit, and the skin on his nose broke open and bled again. He sat in a delicate, high-backed chair and pressed the wound shut while Hannah put fresh sheets on the bed.

In the morning, half asleep, he strolled into the kitchen in his pajamas as usual. Hannah was standing at the door with her back to him, looking out over the frosty garden. Ernest could feel the heat coming off her from twenty feet away. The sky was gray, and it seemed to him that there was no sign of life out there, nothing at all, except for her. Ernest saw the miraculous in my mother, or at least he thought he did. Proof again, I suppose, that we see what we want to see, regardless of what we are actually looking at, nothing at all to do with the truth.

He asked her to stay. He said it out loud before he could think his way out of it. He was tired of being alone. He wanted to live a little, like Margot had told him.

My mother smiled. He expected her to decline politely, to ask him to call her a cab, but she didn't.

She was twenty-one, and he was her ticket out of nowhere.

Hannah never collected her things. Ernest didn't even know if she had any. He didn't meet anyone from her life before—not at the beginning. She started from scratch, like she was brand-new. He had the antique shop in Oxford send the set of glasses, special delivery. Hannah opened the parcel and kissed him. Then she dropped one on the flagstone floor of the kitchen.

"Why would she do that?" I asked.

Ernest shrugged. "She did it on purpose," he told me, "because they were hers now, because she could."

Twelve

Ernest didn't have much time left, but he seemed to have time enough for me. Since Hannah didn't like us being together, we tried finding ways to chat when she was out or asleep, or when her vodka levels kept her from keeping tabs on our conversations. He still thought I was his sister now and then, but I didn't mind so much. In fact, at some point I started to enjoy it while it lasted. Ernest was pretty good company, even when he slipped away on the pain meds and you almost lost him. Even then he had stuff to say that I was interested in hearing.

He slept a lot. And then sometimes he was clearer than others, all there in the room, wide awake and pin sharp, like none of him was sick or weak or missing.

He looked out of his big picture windows, like giant screens where he got to watch live footage of the world. The pale backs of leaves dancing in the last of the sun, the quick fact of a bird on the ledge, low planes overhead, the turned earth in furrowed lines in the fields beyond the garden. Ordinary things, I suppose, but not if you were Ernest, and time was running out, and you didn't know how many chances you'd get to see those things again.

I told him that soon we'd all be able to choose the view from our houses. Soon, our windows would open on all possible virtual worlds and we'd move ourselves from desert island to mountaintop to outer space at the touch of a button.

"And how will we do that?" he said.

"Nano-transformational technology," I said. "You know, like holograms."

"Really?" he said. "In your lifetime?"

"It won't be long," I told him. "Our cars will look like limousines to us if we want them to, a new model, a different color every day. Our roads will be empty, sunlit highways, whatever it is we are driving on, whatever crappy car we drive."

"How so?" he said, and I liked the way he said it. It made me smile.

"Three-dimensional projections," I said. "Hyperreal, interactive illusions."

"Fakes?" he said, and he laughed.

"Yes, fakes," I said. "The real won't be real enough anymore. Only appearances will count."

"Imagine that," he said. "Hannah and Lowell will fit right in."

"Children will be born," I told him, "who'll have no idea that the holograms aren't real, because the holograms will be real, to them. In the end, everyone who remembers a time without them will be dead."

"And what use are the dead to the living?" said Ernest. "They don't even speak the same language."

"You talk to Margot often enough," I said.

"Do I?" He looked surprised. "Must be because I'm nearly there."

Ernest knew he wouldn't be around to see it happen. He'd lived through the beginning of a technological revolution, but he wouldn't see the end. He said he'd try not to judge.

"I've performed my fair share of illusions after all."

Still, he said if he looked out at the night sky through his window and compared it to some future virtual digital recording of the night sky through his window, he wasn't all that sorry to be going.

"In the face of all this mastery of wonder," he said, "I long to rise and glide out, to paraphrase Walt Whitman, to wander off by myself, and from time to time look up in perfect silence at the stars."

"Walt Whitman?" I said.

"Yes. Read him. Read him soon, before I'm gone and the nano-transformers have taken over. Read him in a real-life, actual, rare-as-a-four-leaf-clover *book*."

I promised I would.

He was quiet for a while then, and I sort of knew what he was thinking, so I told him about a thing Thurston and I used to do, a when-I'm-dead game. Thurston started it one night, out of nowhere, when we were out walking.

"When I'm dead," he said, "I'm going to become the skin of an antler, the root of a tooth."

"Can I be an oyster shell?" I said. "The very tip of a tree?"

"We can be anything," Thurston said. "If the mass of the universe never changes, we have to be some part of it when we die."

"Not stars," I said. "I don't want us to be stars."

"No. Let's be paper and subway trains and honey."

"Let's be children's shoes and paintbrushes and lint."

"When I'm dead," he said, "I'm going to take up smoking."

I smiled. "I suppose it can't hurt."

"I'll drive too fast and jump out of airplanes and eat blowfish and poisonous mushrooms. I'll do my best to drink too much and never ever look before I cross the street."

I joined in. "When I'm dead, I'll wear highly flammable clothing and live in a volcano and jump off high buildings and walk across waterfalls on a tightrope."

"We'll be fearless skydivers."

"And swim in shark-infested waters."

"I'll go on an expedition to the North Pole in a T-shirt."

"I'll join a circus and team up with a blind knife thrower."

"I'm almost looking forward to it," Thurston said.

"Don't say that," I told him. "You don't mean that."

When I told Ernest to give it a go, he looked at me for a minute.

"When I'm dead, I will probably sit at my kitchen table with an infinite pack of my old French cigarettes and watch you, whatever it is you're doing."

"That's it?" I said. "A whole world of possibilities, and you want to stay here and look at me?"

"Do you think you'll know if I'm here?" Ernest said. "Maybe you'll smell my tobacco. It's strangely delicious, like burnt leaves and dung."

"Nice."

"If you do, you must look over. You have to say hello."

"What will you say?"

"Oh, nothing much. I'll complain about the lack of good brandy in paradise."

"Paradise? Is that where you're going? Are you sure about that?"

"My wings are still small," he said, smiling and shifting in the bed. "They feel like fists under my skin. They're not ready yet, but they're coming."

Then he asked me if I'd stay here, after he was gone.

Before I could answer he said, "You don't have to, of course. You can do what you want. Sell the place."

"I won't sell your house, Ernest."

"*Your* house."

"Whatever," I told him. "I don't know yet. But I do like it here."

I hadn't thought about what would happen when he was gone. I said so.

"Well, you need to," he said. "That's what's happening. I'm going."

"I know," I said. "You're going. I get it."

Ernest sighed. "And you only just got here."

He'd patrol the grounds while I slept, he said, and check the locks and passages and stairwells for other ghosts and intruders. He'd sit high in the branches of a tree and listen to the night birds, and the cars that sounded, as they passed, like waves on a beach, coming in close and then falling away.

"I won't leave this place if I can help it," he told me. "Not if you're still here. I don't think I could."

I didn't like him saying that. It didn't fit with the way he'd treated me my whole life. It didn't sound honest at all.

"You had no problem leaving me all those years ago," I said, and then I regretted it instantly, because it sounded mean and bitter, even if it was the truth.

He shook his head. "No," he said.

"Yes, Ernest," I said, and I was annoyed suddenly, bubbles of anger popping in my chest. "Do me a favor. Don't say you'll always be here and crap like that, because it's cheap."

"I'm sorry."

"Don't sugarcoat the tiny piece of you I *am* getting," I said.

113

"OK."

"And don't make promises you can't keep," I said. "I don't like it. It's not right."

We made eye contact for a quick second before I looked away. Then he leaned forward a little, closer to me. "Have I told you about *Fire Color One*?"

It was the first time he mentioned it. I'm sure about that.

"*Fire Color One*?" I said. "The Yves Klein painting?"

"Shhh!" He put his hand out. "Not so loud."

"What about it?"

"How much do you know? What have I said?"

"Nothing," I told him. "You haven't said anything. I know what it is, that's all. I know it well."

"You do?"

I have a thing about Yves Klein. I told Ernest so. Klein was important, a visionary, daring and tragic, and ahead of his time.

"For a start, he owned the sky," I said.

Ernest looked out the window at the low gray. "He did?"

"Yes. When he was a kid, he and his friends lay on a beach and divided the elements between them. He got the sky."

"Lucky boy," Ernest said.

"Genius is more like it."

Thurston and I got into the USC Library with fake ID cards (I was 107, he was 93) and we read all about Klein's Zones of Immaterial Pictorial Sensibility. Ernest didn't seem to get it. I had to explain.

"Basically, he got people to pay him gold bullion for nothing."

"Nothing?"

"Well, no, for something—for a moment, for empty space," I said. "He gave them a receipt for it. But if they burned that, he chucked half the gold bullion in the Seine for them too."

"And kept the other half," Ernest said.

"It's brilliant, isn't it? It's genius."

Ernest grinned at me. "Not publicity hungry commercialism, then."

"You know what?" I said. "There was nobody like him. Not then. He couldn't be copied."

"Surely everything can be copied."

"Well, Yves Klein couldn't," I said. "How could anyone copy him when he didn't even touch his own canvases?"

"What?"

"I read it. *He kept a defined and constant distance from the works of art that he created.*"

"Who painted them, then," Ernest asked, "if he didn't?"

I pictured the book, old photos from the sixties.

"His models," I said. "They were his brushes. They were his orchestra. He invited an audience. And he conducted."

"He got pretty girls to cover their naked bodies in paint and press themselves against things?" Ernest said. "You're right, Iris. The man was a genius."

"He looked into the void," I said.

"Whatever that means."

"And he invented a color," I told him. "International Klein Blue. He trademarked it. He covered canvases with solid, uninterrupted color. The same size canvases, the same colors, with different price tags, because they were different moments of creation."

"How do you know the man wasn't a charlatan?"

"Because he brought art out of the airless studio and back to life. He made it immediate. He made it into something more than escape, more than the prison window. He made it exciting and real. He used time and space and wind and rain and fire. He strapped a canvas to the roof of his car and drove to the beach and let the weather make his art for him."

"The prison window," Ernest said. "I like that."

I smiled at him. "I know all about *Fire Color One.*"

"You do?"

The scorched outline of two women, their arms outstretched, like dancers, primitive and elemental. Thurston and I had looked at it in a library book for a long time. I turned the page and there were more photos, black and white and still bristling with something intense and not thought of and new. Thurston said it could have been made especially for me.

"How do you paint with fire?" he said. "How would you do it?"

"With a blowtorch to start," I said, "and then a giant gas-powered fire cannon."

I told Ernest that Yves Klein died suddenly in 1962 when he was only thirty-four. His friends thought he had burned himself up and left a great vacuum. He was a comet, someone said, whose path through life was traced by the scorched empty space he left behind.

Just before he died, he announced that he would produce only "immaterial works" from that point onward, and afterward, people thought he must have known that he was about to become immaterial, about to join the ranks of the dead. They had no other explanation for it than that.

Ernest listened to me intently the whole time I was talking. He didn't take his eyes off me for a second.

"Extraordinary," he said.

"What is?"

"I'm so glad you know a little about art, and the great man."

Then I realized. "You knew all of that already, didn't you?" I said.

Ernest didn't answer me directly. He just said, "Imagine knowing when you're going to die," and I swear there was a new light in his eyes, a quick glimmer. "Just imagine what you could do."

Thirteen

After I destroyed the closet, after the landlord had threat-
ened to evict us, someone told Hannah and Lowell that
they had to take me to the fire station. They marched me
down there, barking like dogs, hauled me up in front of
the first fireman they could find. His name was Collins,
the uncle of a boy I knew at school.

"I made an appointment," Hannah said, like that was
a proper substitute for "hello."

He shifted on his feet. "We usually do groups," he
said, "class visits, not individual children."

"She's homeschooled," said Lowell, which was a lie,
but convincing enough, especially with the twenty-dollar
bill he showed him. "Make an exception."

I could see Andrew Jackson's face on Lowell's twenty, the seventh president of the United States, a slave trader, by the way, who engineered genocide against the Native American people and profited from the repossession of their land. Maybe it's an honor a man like that doesn't deserve, but then again, sometimes I think the best place for him is stuck on the front of a twenty for all eternity. The guy must have really loved money.

Lowell palmed the bill like a dealer and passed it over in a handshake. He got a kick out of doing that, I could tell.

Officer Collins had a short brown beard, thick and blunt-cut like a doormat, and huge red hands like cuts of meat. At the sound of my mother's voice, three or four other firemen had wandered out into the yard from the back room. They stood like Collins's back line and watched. Finally he took the money, pocketed it, looked at Lowell, and nodded.

"Five minutes," he said.

Hannah yanked me into place.

"These men," she yelled, "are going to tell you what's what. So help me God, you'd better be listening."

She and Lowell went to wait in the car, Hannah's sandals slapping across the yard like flat hands. Officer Collins kept his eyes on the ground. I'm not sure he appreciated my family's feel for drama. Either that or he knew I'd just seen how much he cost. He smiled at me, smoothed his wire-haired face down from top to bottom, and sighed, "Let's go."

I followed him down a lightless corridor that smelled of old sneakers and rubber and sweat.

"Fire is not a game," he said over his shoulder, and I nodded and tried to keep my face straight. I was too old for this. "A small fire can grow into a deadly fire in just one or two minutes."

He told me these things the same way I used to practice my spelling from start to finish—without thinking—because I'd done it a thousand times before, because I had to.

I could have been anyone. Officer Collins didn't seem to care.

"Never play with matches or lighters or gas," he said. I wondered if he was curious why I was playing with any of it at all.

He showed me all the equipment, the suits and masks hanging empty, the idle flat hose, the stacked-up breathing apparatus, the parked truck. It was a disappointment, frankly. There was next to nothing going on. The firemen that I saw were watching TV, playing cards, killing time. I wondered if they ever wanted a fire to happen, the same way I did, just for something to break the monotony, just for something to do. I had my fingers crossed behind my back that the alarms would sound, that they'd leap up like superheroes, that I'd get to see them in action, but they didn't—I didn't. They stayed slumped at tables, catnapping on couches, scratching, smoking, and eating. It smelled of burnt bacon and stale sweat in there.

Officer Collins gave me a bunch of sad leaflets. They said MEET BUZZY THE SMOKE DETECTOR! and I'M SPLASH THE FIRE EXTINGUISHER! They said NEVER COOK IN LONG SLEEVES! and WHY NOT PRACTICE YOUR OWN FIRE DRILL? I pictured myself putting a match to them. I imagined them flowering to ash in my hand. I'd have liked to give him some leaflets of my own. DON'T PATRONIZE A PYROMANIAC!! and DON'T UNDERESTIMATE A QUIET KID WITH A LIGHTER!!! and DON'T SPEND THAT $20 ON FRIED MEAT, FATSO!!

Back out in the yard, he put his face level with mine. Up close, I could see the tiny holes in his skin where the hairs grew, like wet clay pushing through a sieve.

"Young lady, I hear you had some trouble with a fire," he said.

I shrugged. "I don't know. It was an accident. It was no trouble."

He looked at the sky and laughed. I could see where his teeth had gone brown, right at the back of his mouth.

"I'm going to make a deal with you," he said. "If you don't strike a match or play with fire for the next two weeks, if you can

122

come back and say you haven't done that, then you can ride with us in the fire truck, if you'd like to."

I didn't say anything.

"Wouldn't you like to?" he said.

I shook my head. "Not so much."

"Haven't you ever thought about being a firefighter yourself?"

I stared him down.

"You see a lot of fires that way." Officer Collins leaned back a little, like a fisherman, reeling me in. "You get up real close. You do it again and again and again."

I kept my mouth shut. I wore my poker face, and when Hannah and Lowell called me over, I walked slow and steady to the car.

Two weeks is a long time to go without a thing when you have a craving for it. The whole world was tempting me to fail, leaving cigarettes burning in ashtrays, matches on the sidewalk, dropping lighters from pockets, from bags. Everywhere I looked, there was a trap someone had set for me, like they'd read the stupid safety leaflets and decided to do the exact opposite. But that fire truck was waiting, scrubbed and shined and gleaming, just around the corner. Maybe this was what I wanted—to become a firefighter myself. I told Thurston. I said it was worth trying for and I was going to try damn hard. I wanted to speed through the streets in that thing, its siren wailing, its bulk shifting underneath me, its lights flashing danger and rescue all at once. If I was one of them, I could get as close to a fire as I dared and it would be OK, it'd be my job. I'd get paid for it, and get up every morning and do it again.

For two long weeks, I ignored the matches and the cigarette butts and the naked flames. For fourteen days and nights, I sat on my hands and didn't try to find out what a box of dolls looked like on fire, or a shoe, or a stack of magazines left out with the trash, damp and covered in bat shit. I walked past all of those things with my face turned away. And when it was over, I went back down to the fire station. Nobody needed to march me there this time. I was glad to go.

There was still nothing much happening. They were all still lounging around like fed dogs, time wasting, cooking sausages, dozing. It was like Sleeping Beauty's castle in there. Officer Collins didn't even get up off his butt, and he wouldn't look at me, either, not straight on.

He cleared his throat in his big old easy chair and said, "Look, kid, we're pretty busy."

"But you told me," I said. "You said if I—"

"What's your name again?"

I glared at him. "Iris."

"That's right," he said. "Iris. Did you get caught smoking? Was that you?"

"No," I told him. "I don't smoke."

He shrugged. "Come by next open day and maybe you can climb up inside and take a look."

"What's this, now?" one of the others asked him.

I said we had a deal that I could ride in the truck.

He laughed, punching Collins on the arm. "You gotta stop that, Joe. How many kids you promised this month?"

Collins grinned. "I lost count."

It didn't matter what I said. He wasn't keeping his promise, however hard I'd worked to keep mine. A ride in a fire truck didn't seem to mean a thing to him, one way or the other. Like the saying goes, you don't know what you've got until it's gone.

Thurston was waiting for me when I got home. He was sitting on the wall outside my apartment building.

"How'd it go?" he said.

I looked at him. "They lied to me," I said. "I don't want to talk about it."

I left him there on the wall, and I went inside and sulked in my room. I could hear the neighbors' washed sheets snapping outside

125

like sails in the wind. It was a hot dry day, and it hadn't rained in a while. I lay on my bed and listened to the sirens in my head. Any minute, I was going to get up, get a few things together, sneak out, and light the mother of all fires, fourteen days' worth, behind the tiny parched yard out back. Nobody would see me. I was going to light three, starting in the far corner and moving in. The wind would pick them up and pull them together, and I'd be back inside by the time anyone noticed a thing. Those sheets would be gray with soot before the neighbors could take them down.

I was still lying there when Thurston came around the back of the building and threw a handful of stones against my window. The sirens in my head were suddenly real, suddenly outside. I looked out and he bowed, like a man on a stage, and offered me the view with a sweep of his arm. What I'd been thinking about, Thurston had been doing, quiet as a cat. That dried-out stretch of land was leaping, wild red and crackling, the heat coming off it like surf, flames lapping against the garages and summerhouses, pooling at the edge of the ground-floor properties. I don't know how many people had dialed 911. Their phones must have been ringing off the hook. I stood at my window and watched the fire trucks come, more than one, sirens on, lights blazing, filled to the brim with superheroes dressed in hard hats and fat trousers and bug-eyed masks. I stayed out of sight, and I watched those lazy, good-for-nothing, promise-breaking, bacon-crammed firemen as they battled with the flames. Nobody was hurt. They lost a couple of verandas to the fire, and an old disused pickup, and someone's trellis, someone else's doghouse. They lost a few gallons in sweat, I'd say, as well, and maybe a pound or two in weight.

Thurston stood behind the barrier, watching with the rest of the small crowd, blending in, wearing just the right mask of shock and awe on his face.

Thank you, I mouthed at him through the glass when he looked up.

He blew me a kiss. *You're welcome,* it said.

When the fire had been put out and the crowds had gone, I went down to find him. He was waiting for me across the road. I hugged him hard. I hadn't done it before, but I didn't think twice about it. He smelled of kerosene and charcoal, and I breathed him in.

"I can't believe you just did that."

"I'd do anything for you," Thurston said, and he hugged me back. "I thought you knew that already."

I didn't want to let go. I really didn't. "I feel the same about you."

Thurston had my back. He was the only one who did.

Fourteen

Ernest said that the tree outside his window arrived years ago from Holland, on Margot's twelfth birthday. A black pear, already twenty feet high, more than eight feet around; he said its root ball alone weighed almost three tons. The men stopped on the road with it strapped down like Gulliver in the bed of their truck. Passing drivers slowed to make sense of what they were seeing, caught a glimpse of the prone giant, and then were gone.

"We ran outside," Ernest said, "and there it was, a tree on its side, made from ravens and dragons, its thick bark crackled with scales, the buds of its leaves smooth and solid as claws."

He and Margot invaded the tree like termites. Their mom watched with her arms folded and her mouth stretched in a thin straight line before she called them inside and scolded them for playing near the road.

Margot fumed.

"But it's a lying-down tree," she said.

"And it's Margot's birthday," Ernest added. "We thought it was for her."

Their mother didn't soften. She sent them upstairs to wash their hands and think about what they'd done.

"What would you do with your own tree anyway?" Ernest asked.

"Climb it," Margot said. "Carve my name in it with a knife, lean against its trunk in the shade, eat its fruit." She sighed. "So much better than a doll."

He said she'd slouched into the nursery that morning trailing the new doll after her, bumping it along the floorboards. She'd dragged the thing in by its long corn-yellow hair.

"What am I going to do with *this*?" she asked.

Ernest sniggered. "Tie it to some train tracks," he suggested. "Shoot it with arrows. Gouge out its eyes and fill its head with birdseed."

Margot grinned. "Drown it in a cattle trough," she said. "Set fire to its hair."

And then the tree had arrived, he said, and the doll was forgotten, left on the floor with one eye shut and its polka-dot dress pulled up over its head while the children pressed their faces flat against the windows to get a better view.

He sat up in bed and looked out while he told me.

"The crane driver sat in his cab," he said, pointing, "and when the tree lifted, it came up headfirst and then just hung there, strangely upright, like it was planted in midair."

It cast a shadow over all the rooms they ran through, a great dark beast flying past the house. It blocked out the sun, the birds stopped singing, and downstairs someone dropped a plate on the flagstone floor.

The men dug a crater on the east side of the house, a great scar of a bowl, the turf cut open and pulled back over itself like so much skin. Ernest said it looked as if the moon had fallen right out of the sky and landed in their garden. Margot wanted more than anything to crouch at the bottom of that hole and look up at the sky. She saw herself lying out there in the cool, upturned earth, like buried treasure, with her spine pressed into the ground like a worm and the shadows of birds gliding across her face.

"Don't even think about it," said their mom, one hand resting on the back of Margot's neck.

"Of course it was too late," Ernest said. "She already had."

Margot and Ernest weren't allowed to get their hands dirty, not that day. They sprawled across the nursery floor like late bees, dying of boredom. The tree was lying slain in the garden and the men had stopped for lunch. In a fit of caution, their mom had locked the doors. Nobody was allowed outside until the thing was staked and planted. They still didn't know where the tree had come from, or why it had been brought to their house, and she didn't trust it not to roll or break or fall. She didn't trust the men to know what they were doing, either. Ernest's dad called her a catastrophist. He said Margot would get cabin fever, but not Ernest of course, her houseplant child, her rare orchid.

Ernest was trying to make the perfect spit bubble. Margot said it was the worst birthday ever. They lay on their backs, staring at a crack in the ceiling until their vision blurred and the crack swam around and disappeared.

Margot said, "I want to bury something. Let's hide treasure under the tree for someone to dig up in five hundred years. What have we got that's good enough?"

They packed everything neatly into a black metal box, locked it and spread out the keys: they left one in the lock, to be helpful, and one above the picture frame in the nursery. Margot climbed on top of the toy chest to put it there.

Ernest still remembered the things they'd buried like it was yesterday. While he was telling me, he looked down at his lap as if they were spread out on the bed in front of him, as if he could see them all. A pocket mirror, the front page of the newspaper, Margot's silver christening cup. Ernest's wounded toy soldiers. A photo of both of them together. A feather, an old medicine bottle containing one of Ernest's baby teeth, some of Margot's hair, and a drop of each of their blood. Margot cut Ernest's thumb with her whittling knife and said, "Who knows what they'll be able to tell about us in the future from these samples? They might make new ones of us altogether. We'll wake up in a lab in a thousand years and get to live our lives all over again."

Ernest wanted to know if he'd remember his first life—this one—the one where they had buried the stuff.

"Probably," Margot said. "But mostly we'll remember the hundreds of years of waiting under that tree."

"I didn't want to do that," he told me. Ernest said he started to snivel, but Margot told him to be brave, in the interests of future science.

Work started up again. The tree was airborne, swinging into position.

It was her idea, she said, so it should be her job to bury the treasure.

Ernest watched from the window while Margot skipped down the back stairs, took the spare key from the hook in the kitchen, and was gone.

"By the time anyone else saw her," he said, "it was almost too late."

The crane screamed in its efforts to stop the tree from crashing down on top of her. There was a great screeching of brakes and a grinding of metal on metal and then the shouts of the men got louder. Ernest said his mom ran out of the house, shrieking and tearing at her hair, white as a sheet. She looked seasick; everyone did. Only Margot looked overjoyed and defiant, beaming, her arms and legs stuck with mud as she climbed out of the crater, the tree's roots swaying like snakes in the air less than six feet above her head. Her dad slapped her face, and Ernest burst into tears, but Margot didn't stop smiling.

She was sent to bed without dinner. She was officially in trouble. Ernest would have been punished just for talking to her.

Later that night, he crept quietly to her room. "Why didn't you just throw the box in?" he asked her through the bedroom door.

"Where's the fun in that?" she said. "I had to lie down in there, the way I pictured it, or the box would have seen what I never got to see."

"A tree, coming to crush you to death?"

"Exactly," hissed Margot. "It was terrifying. It was amazing."

"But it was so dangerous," he said. "You could've been killed."

"Haven't you figured it out yet?" Margot asked him.

"What?"

"Life's big secret. If a thing's not dangerous, it's hardly worth doing."

"That can't be true," he said.

"Oh, but it is."

"Mother is going to kill you," he told her.

Margot was tired of the conversation. He could hear it in her voice. "Don't be silly, Ernest. That's precisely the last thing she's ever going to do. Mother is all about keeping us alive, at the expense of anyone having any actual fun."

"What does that mean?"

"Do you remember the last time we were really high up on the ridge in the wind and Mother panicked and told us all not to look down? Well, she was wrong. I looked down, and the view was unbelievable."

Ernest looked at me and smiled.

"Margot said, 'What's the point of being up there if you're not going to look down? What's the point of doing anything at all?'"

I watched him lying there, old before his time and new to me and nearly gone.

"Is that what you believe?" I said. "Do you think Margot was right?"

Ernest sighed. "I hope so," he said. "You remind me so much of her. Brave and opinionated and reckless. She lived a better life than me. I hope to God you do too."

Fifteen

Hannah continued to watch Ernest and me pretty closely. She really didn't like us spending time together, not without her there. Guaranteed, after less than five minutes, her footsteps would echo up the stairs or she'd call my name from somewhere else in the house. I wasn't used to it, my mother minding where I was. It made me feel uncomfortable.

And she was behaving strangely. That morning, I'd caught the faint, acrid scent of burnt paper and found her standing over it, a slack heap of flame in an ashtray.

"Did you do this?" she asked, when we both knew that, for a change, I hadn't.

"She's anxious about her inheritance," I said to Ernest.

"Of course she is," he said. "She wouldn't be Hannah if she wasn't."

Fluid from his lungs was draining into a bag. It was the color of mustard water, cloudy and adrift like a lava lamp. Without that bag, he'd have drowned.

"She'll be furious if you leave me everything."

"I know," he said.

"So give it all to her," I told him. "I don't need anything."

He smiled. "I'm waiting for her to persuade me. She doesn't like being upstaged by her daughter."

"I'm not upstaging anyone," I said.

"Yes, you are," he said, and his throat sounded thick and hoarse. "And what's worse, you're not even trying."

"I don't want to try."

"Even more infuriating. Your mother is used to being the center of attention."

"Lowell's worse," I said, and he looked unconvinced. "I mean it. Seriously."

I told him that Lowell spent even more time in front of a mirror than Hannah did. He was the first to wilt if nobody was looking at him, like a plant in a drought. He lasted two minutes and twenty-eight seconds in a room alone before he picked up the

137

phone and called somebody so he could talk about himself. I knew that for a fact because I'd timed him. Two twenty-eight was his personal best.

Ernest's laugh was like stones landing in a puddle. "She met her match, then."

"I don't know about that." I'd always wondered what there was for her to like about Lowell, once she'd gotten used to his handsome, predictable face.

Ernest said, "Have you ever met her family?"

I shook my head. "I didn't think there was any," I said. "I figured she was born out of an egg."

"They were poor," he said. "I know that much. I worked that much out for myself."

"Well, she loves money enough."

"It saved her," he said.

"Depends which way you look at it."

He smiled. "She never liked how you and I got along."

"Us?" I said. "We did?"

"Like a house on fire," he said, and I tried not to blush, but felt my cheeks flaming up anyway.

"I don't remember," I told him.

"But I do," Ernest said.

He closed his eyes while the nurse shut off the tube in his side and covered it with a clean dressing.

Hannah insisted I help with the inventory and everything, and I had to give it to her, she was right about one thing: Ernest's collection was incredible. I didn't pay much attention to the dining-room cabinets, but I did walk through the rooms making a list of all the art. Ernest must have been proud of the beautiful things he'd filled his house with, centuries of them, old masters and impressionists and modernists silently preening on his walls. I told him so. I said I wished Thurston could be here. He'd have been so happy to get that close without an alarm sounding, without three security guards removing him from the building. He'd tried to touch a Basquiat at MOCA when he was a kid. He hardly moved before they stopped him, grown men with static radios and steel-cap shoes.

"It was a thoughtcrime," he said. "And the second time I tried, I was out. My feet didn't touch the ground."

"Do you have a favorite? From my collection?" Ernest asked me, but I didn't. How was I supposed to compare them? It wasn't possible. But I could at least be honest about it.

"You should know we're logging everything," I said. "I think

Hannah's getting ready for the biggest yard sale of all time."

He leaned forward and pinched the bridge of his nose with his fingers.

"She's done that before," he said.

"When?"

"Years ago. Your mother likes to be in control of things."

"No shit," I told him. "I've met her too, you know."

"Iris!" Just then we heard her from somewhere downstairs.

He laughed. "And she wants to control what we talk about."

He shifted in his bed. I got up and rearranged his pillows. "Better," he whispered. "Thank you."

Ernest said Hannah was afraid of the things he knew, things she wouldn't want him to tell me.

"Like what?"

"My story," he said. "My version of the truth."

"So why would she bring me," I said, "if she had stuff to hide?"

"Money," he said. "The prize. Don't underestimate its hold over her. Your mother will stop at nothing to get it."

"You think?" I said, smiling.

"And she didn't expect me to last this long. I don't think she planned for us to meet at all."

"True," I said. "She kind of hoped you'd be dead when we got here."

"Your mother never liked to wait for things."

"So when are you going to tell me your version?" I said. "You're going to, right?"

"Iris?" We could hear Hannah's voice on the stairs, getting louder. "Iris!"

"Three and a half minutes," I said. "She's getting quicker."

"You'll know everything," he said. "As soon as it's safe for you to know."

"*Fire Color One*," I said. "Tell me about that."

"Not now," he told me. "Not in front of her."

My mother pushed into the room, loud and breathless, looking from me to him and back again like she'd be able to tell by our faces how much had been said.

"I need you in the kitchen," she said. "And I'm sure Ernest could use a break from your chatter."

I stayed right where I was. "I'll be down in a minute."

"No," she said, gripping the door with both hands, white-knuckled with stress and boredom and the slow passing of time. "*You'll go now.*"

She was beginning to show signs of going too long without a

copy of *Vogue* or an eyebrow wax. The polish on her nails was beginning to chip. Her hair looked kind of greasy. It was only a matter of time before she'd have to go back to the city.

"An egg, you say?" Ernest said, and he winked at me and sank back into his pillows. I could see he was in pain, and it occurred to me that he hadn't taken his morphine, not that I noticed, not while he was with me. Maybe he did need a rest.

A vein in Hannah's temple was pulsing. Her eyes burned laser holes into my sweatshirt, willing me to leave. I got up slowly, to annoy her more than anything.

"See you later," I said.

Ernest waved and Hannah shut the door on me, shut herself in the room with him, and turned the key in the door. I wasn't expecting that. It occurred to me then that she could step right up and play the Grim Reaper herself if she just had five minutes with him on her own. It was a terrible thing to think about my own mother, but it had the ring of truth about it all the same.

I stayed where I was. Outside his bedroom. I had this dumb idea about trying to protect him. If anything happened, I could beat the door down or go and get Dawn. And I was curious too. I wanted to listen to what they were saying.

I wondered what it was like between the two of them now, my mother and my dad.

So I deserved to hear what I did. Standing on the wrong side of that locked door in the quiet, I suddenly realized Hannah was ramping up the competition, playing me to win. And like the cage fighter she was underneath that glossy surface, she didn't care how low down she went to do it.

Sixteen

My mother was pacing Ernest's room in her high heels, with her loping walk. Her shoes were loud as hammers on the wooden boards. I pictured her reading charts or dialing up the morphine dosage or getting ready to switch something vital off or up or down. When she finally sat down, I heard the sigh and shush of her skirt riding up, her legs crossing and uncrossing, Hannah-style, and I heard my own heartbeat, pulsing away in the quiet of the hall. I'll bet she ran her hand up and down her arm and gave him her best look too.

She must have done something like that, because Ernest laughed, just a little. "We're way past that, Hannah," he said. "Just tell me what you want."

"We need to talk about Iris," she said.

Ernest's breath sounded like that last little drop of soda being pulled through a straw. "What is there to say?"

"She seems pleased to see you."

"I think we're doing OK."

"Don't be fooled," she told him, and every cell of my body went on high alert.

"By what? By Iris?"

"I don't think you can trust her."

Ernest waited. I counted to three before he said, "What is this, Hannah?"

"She's dangerous," my mother said. "She could hurt you."

I went cold all over. I wanted to bang on the door and have my say, but I didn't even move. I just stood there.

"Believe me," Ernest told her. "Nothing is getting through this morphine wall."

"You don't understand," Hannah said. "Iris isn't right."

I pressed my head against the wall and tried to breathe.

"What in God's name are you talking about?" said Ernest.

"I'm talking about arson," she whispered, like saying it any louder could make it happen.

She wasn't lying. I couldn't exactly deny it.

"Arson?"

"You can't let Iris near matches or anything like that," Hannah said.

"You're serious?"

"She'll burn the place down as soon as look at you."

"Why are you telling me this now?" Ernest said.

"I'm worried about you with her here. I can't sleep or even think straight, I'm so worried about your safety."

"My safety's not really an issue," he said. "If I die tomorrow, it's only a few days ahead of schedule."

"And the paintings?" she said.

"Ah," he said. "That's more like it. The paintings. Don't you worry, Hannah. They're insured."

"They're irreplaceable," she said. "You know that."

"And?"

"And I think we should move them now."

"Where to?"

"I don't know. An auction house, proper storage. Somewhere else."

Ernest groaned. I heard him. His voice was small and flat and defeated. "I don't think we need to do that."

"If Iris starts one of her fires," Hannah told him, "we won't get

146

you out of here quick enough. You'll go off like a bomb with all this oxygen in the room."

I had this idea that my mother was going to torch the place and then blame it on me. It rushed through me like a blast of cold air.

"Not such a bad way to go," he told her.

"She set fire to my bedroom," Hannah said. "And our apartment building. She set fire to her school, for God's sake. She's out of control. She won't stop."

"Why didn't you say something before?" Ernest asked. "Why did you bring her here if she's such a threat?"

"You told me to," she said. "You wanted it."

I could almost taste it, his disapproval, of her or of me, I wasn't sure. Maybe it was both.

"That mattered all of a sudden, did it?" he said. "What I wanted?"

"We left the States," she told him, "because Iris burned us out. People were threatening to sue. She was this close to getting arrested, or committed, or both."

Neither of them spoke. I stood still in the quiet, hardly breathing, hearing even the sound my eyelids made when I blinked. I knew I wasn't the only reason we'd left, but I also knew there was nothing I could do or say right then to save myself. I should have been the one to tell him. What must he think of me now?

"Do you understand what I'm saying?" said Hannah.

"She lights fires." Ernest sounded far away, like he'd been punching the morphine button.

"She's dangerous."

He breathed out slowly and deliberately. "What do you want from me, Hannah?" he said.

She stood up again and walked across the room.

Ernest asked, "What does your boyfriend say?"

"Nothing," Hannah told him. "He says nothing useful at all."

"About Iris? Or about everything?"

"Don't change the subject, Ernest," she said.

"Tell me what you want."

"I need to borrow some money," she said, "to take care of her."

I should have seen it coming. With my mother, all roads led to that. Hannah would tap him for a few thousand, not for a private facility or a hospital or a school, but to get herself out of Dodge, away from her creditors. My mother wouldn't throw good money after something bad like me.

"Well, I have plenty of money," Ernest told her. "You know that."

"And let me have the paintings," she cooed. "I'll take care of them."

I could hear the smile in her voice.

Ernest sighed heavily. "You should have come back before now," he said. "We might have salvaged something."

"You and me?" Hannah said.

"No. Me and Iris."

My mother continued on without missing a beat. "You know what your collection means to me," she whispered.

"It means money to you," he said. "I think with Iris it's about the art."

She licked her lips. I heard her.

"Why should I believe a word you say?" Ernest asked her.

"I'm not a monster," Hannah told him. "I am your wife and the mother of your child. Whatever else has passed between us, I am the woman who has given you that."

They were quiet in there for a moment and then Ernest said, "I want to leave Iris some things from my collection. What can I give her?"

"Just leave her one painting," Hannah said. "Give her that new one. It's not my thing."

"Just one?" he said.

"Leave the rest of them to me," she said. "I wouldn't trust Iris with anything that hasn't already burned down."

Seventeen

I didn't wait for them to finish talking. I ran down the
back stairs to the old kitchen, and I cried for exactly one
minute, out of anger more than anything. I went through
the house like a bug bomb, in and out of everything, picking up anything that could start a fire, cramming it all
into my pockets. I emptied Hannah's handbag. I took her
lighter and her cigarettes, and her phone too, just to piss
her off. Then I came out to get my bike. It was leaning up
against the woodpile. I tried not to think about that neatly
stacked firewood wall splitting and burning and caving
in on itself in a heap of fire and rage and ash. I grabbed
a stack of old newspapers and a jar of turpentine I found
in a shed. I took my bike straight to the other side of the

woods, crashed it across long fields and through wet grass and down bone-rattling paths.

I didn't want Ernest hearing that stuff about me. Not from her. I knew what knowing it would do. I thought I could hear it in his voice already—judgment and distance. He would wash his hands of me all over again. Who wants to have a problem child? Not him. Not a man who didn't want to be a father in the first place.

I kicked out a big dip in the soft ground with my heels and filled it with dust-dry leaves and snaps of kindling. I struck a match. It made my heartbeat pop like a hit of strong caffeine, like an adrenaline shot. I put the flame to a clutch of dead and tangled grass, dropped it on a nest of papers. It flickered and spread. I crossed cuttings and small branches like a lattice across the top of the bowl, like the bars of a cage, and the fire ate through them, hungry as hell. The air got thick and sharp, and my eyes watered. When I dragged some of the larger branches onto the flames and sprinkled them with turpentine, they cracked and sighed and blackened as the thing began to take hold. For a while I stopped thinking. It started to get dark, and I was doing a pretty good job of clearing the forest floor of anything fit to burn. It looked like a swept carpet. The fire was huge. They must have heard it booming and crackling from inside the house. They would have seen its vengeful

151

halo glow, flinging light and shadows out across the fields. I wondered if they watched, or drew the curtains and turned their backs on it. That would be the difference between us.

All night I dragged fallen branches and scrub and clusters of hissing spruce onto the flames. I didn't stop to rest or think. It took up all the air and space and noise in my head. I was trying to burn my mind clean with it.

I knew what it looked like, knew I was playing straight into my mother's hands by playing with fire, that I wasn't doing anything to help myself in Ernest's eyes, but honestly, I couldn't stop myself. Let Ernest think what he liked. It was too late now anyway.

And he'd never understand, so there was no point in explaining. No point in telling him I find it near impossible to look anywhere else when there's a fire burning. That it dips and flares and travels and breathes—a living thing—and it occupies me completely. I think about how old it is, this scrap of magic, this creator and destroyer, how fundamental and miraculous, how constant and opposite. He wouldn't understand why I think about the dancing, shifting, elusive character of a fire, of the colors it paints, unlike any other colors I will ever find, in a whole lifetime of looking. That I am seduced by it. How it gets me every time.

Eighteen

In the morning, Hannah came to find me. I heard her moving through the woods before I saw her. I heard the broken cereal crunch of leaves and snapped twigs under her feet. I hadn't slept. My fire was still smoldering, and I was still angry. So was she. The walk through the forest had messed up her hair and ruined her shoes.

"How could you?" I said.

She glared at me, one part concerned mother, two parts war. "Ernest deserves to hear the truth."

"Why?" I said, and I found it hard to look at her. "What good does it do?"

"That's hardly the point."

I couldn't stand the thought of him lying there in his

room, knowing all this about me. I wondered what else I was supposed to feel, apart from fury and disappointment, apart from shame.

I should have told him myself. She should have let me.

"What was the point of bringing me out here?" I said. "If you were just going to turn him against me, why did I have to come?"

Hannah didn't answer. She just stood there picking bits of leaf and twig off the front of her sweater.

"You ruined everything," I said. "You are such a bitch."

She smiled. "Well, there you are—you both probably still agree on something."

I wiped my hands down the sides of my jeans, wiped my face with my sleeve. I was shaking. My fire wasn't working, not anymore. I didn't feel calm, or empty, or better. I wanted to scream. I wanted to run. I wanted to hit her. If Thurston had been there, he'd have held on to me and talked me down. He would have understood me, even if nobody else did.

"Anyway," my mother said, "Ernest wants to talk to you."

"What for?" I said.

She stood there with her arms folded, drumming her long fingers on her own elbows. "How should I know?"

I didn't move.

"Are you coming, or aren't you?" she asked me.

I shrugged. "I don't know."

"Well, I'm not waiting," she said, brushing her palms together, scratching at her neck, reaching up to fix her hair. "This place is crawling."

"So go," I said. "I didn't ask you to come and get me."

"No," she said. "*He* did."

When she left, I watched her disappear through the trees, and it hit me for the first time just how tired I was of all of it, of being here and being alone and trying to stay upright, trying to be so damn strong. I didn't think I had any fight left in me, so I gave up. I got my bike and went back to the house. I couldn't stay by the fire forever, and I had no idea what else I was supposed to do. I stamped out the last embers, but I didn't catch up and walk with her. I didn't overtake, even though I knew a quicker way. I just stayed behind at a safe distance, like you do when you track a wild animal, because you can never be sure when they are going to turn on you and let down their claws and attack.

I brought the smell of fire into Ernest's room, the proof of my guilt, right there in the air around us. I'd washed my hands and face, but my clothes still stank. Hannah went ahead of me up the stairs, and when we walked in, he didn't take any notice, not at first. Dawn was shaving him without disturbing the oxygen tube that ran between his upper lip and nose like a mustache, keeping his blood fed, given his lungs' reluctance to do so. He didn't say a word until she was finished, and when he did speak, he sounded bone weary. You could hear it.

"Ladies. Leave us, please."

Dawn went first, but my mother stayed put with her hands on her hips.

"Are you sure?" she said.

Ernest waved her away with his hand.

"Go and cash your check, Hannah," he said. "You've got what you wanted. Now give me my turn."

She thought about arguing, I watched her think it through, and then she backed out, closing the door behind her. Outside, a breeze brushed through the trees. Birds trilled and whistled. Somewhere I could hear a tractor, the odd car passing. Other than that, the silence between us felt like lead injected straight into the air. Ernest broke it first.

"Margot was like you," he said. "She felt better when something was burning."

I didn't say anything.

"Cleaner and calmer," he said. "That's what she told me, something like that."

I emptied my pockets onto the table by the window—matches and lighters and rags and sticks and old paper. I said I was sorry he hadn't heard it from me.

"We all have our secrets," he told me. "I wouldn't blame you for that."

I should have said I wouldn't blame him then, for leaving me alone my whole life, but I held it in. I kept it to myself. I still feel bad about that.

"Are you worried now," I asked him. "About your stuff? About your collection and everything, with me here?"

"Should I be?"

I shook my head. "I wouldn't do anything to damage your paintings, or hurt you," I said.

Ernest smiled. "I didn't think so."

"If there's a fire inside this house, I swear it won't be because of me."

"I know," he said. "I believe you."

"I don't know why she told you," I said. "She didn't have to do that."

"*Radix malorum est cupiditas.*"

"What the hell does that mean?"

"The love of money is the root of all evil."

"Yep," I said. "You got that right."

Ernest let out a breath, and it hurt him. I could see how much it hurt. I looked around the room.

"Are you ashamed of me?" I said. "Am I a disappointment?"

"Not at all," he said. "Don't think that."

"I wouldn't blame you for feeling that way," I said. "I really wouldn't."

Ernest shifted himself in the bed. "I could ask you the same thing."

"I used to know how I'd answer," I said. "I don't anymore."

He studied my face for a second. Then he said, "What did Hannah tell you, about me?"

"Nothing good. Why?"

"I just wondered what you knew."

I looked around the room because I couldn't look at him. There were three photos of me on the dresser, silver-framed Irises aged one and two and three. I hadn't noticed them before.

"She said you weren't cut out to be a father," I told him. "She said the whole children thing left you cold."

"Not true."

"She said you weren't interested. She said you threw us out and knew where we were the whole time but you chose never to contact us."

He shook his head. His voice was cracked and swallowed, but he got the words out in the end. "She's lying, Iris. So many damn lies."

Those pictures you see of people who have spontaneously combusted, those old, black-and-white photos of a pipe and slippers and just a heap of ash—I was about to become one of those. I could feel it. Any minute now, I would be nothing but dust.

Ernest's skin was dull like wax, beaded with sweat. He pressed the button for his morphine, three times. He looked up at the ceiling. His eyes kept closing. He dropped off for about twenty seconds and then his breathing stopped and he woke right back up again with a start, like something made him jump.

"It was impossible," he said. "So I gave up."

"What was impossible? Being my dad?"

"All the questions I asked," he said, "and the people I paid, who tried and failed."

"What do you mean," I asked him, *"people you paid*? What are you talking about?"

"I would have traced them," he told me, words slurring slightly, "but they changed their names."

"Ernest," I told him, "look at me. I'm Iris, OK? I'm not Margot. Do you know that?"

He looked at me sideways, moving only his eyes. He didn't turn his head.

"Funny," he said. "If *Lowell* had found any kind of success as an actor, I'd have found you."

"Were you looking for me?" I said, and I felt this thundering in my chest, like horses' hooves, like the spilling lip of a waterfall.

Ernest closed his eyes again. He spoke without opening them. "For over twelve years. One hundred and forty-six months. Six hundred and thirty-two weeks."

I moved closer to him, dragging the old smell of burning halfway across his room.

"Four thousand, four hundred and twenty-six days, to be precise," he said.

"You counted?" I asked him, and something bloomed in my head when I said it, something like wonder, or relief.

He nodded. "Where did they get the name Baxter from anyway?" he said, like I would know. "A can of soup?"

"What are you saying?" I asked. "They changed their names? Why would they do that?"

Ernest was quiet for a moment. I think he was deciding on the right words. High up in my chest, I felt the buzz and flap of wings, like a flock of birds, or those hillsides thick with butterflies, or a swarm of bees.

"So I wouldn't find them," he said. "So I wouldn't find you."

"But they didn't want me," I said. "Not really."

"No. But I did."

I think I steadied myself at the foot of his bed. I think I looked down at my fingers clinging on there. I remember feeling like I wasn't in the room, not anymore, and also that I'd never been more present in my life.

"You weren't the only thing they stole from me," Ernest said, and he turned his face to the window, "but you were the most precious."

I sat down beside him. I saw the shape of his legs under the covers, thin and wasted.

"So all this time . . ."

"Yes, Iris."

"Have I been here before?" I said. "In this house? In this room?"

Ernest's eyes were still closed. "This was your home," he said, "for the first three years of your life. And it's your home now."

161

I shook my head, confused, full of questions. "If they did this to you—" I said.

"To us," he interrupted.

"Then why the hell would they come here? Why would they bring me back?"

He shrugged. "I've asked myself the same thing."

"And . . ."

"I think they ran out of rope. That, and money. When they left, they drained the bank account I set up for you when you were first born. They must have finally run out and couldn't make ends meet. Had nowhere left to turn."

"And you were ill," I said.

"A real gift horse," Ernest added. "A real piece of good luck, for them."

He was paler than ever, contorted somehow against the pain.

"Call the nurse," he said. "I'm sorry. This is unbearable."

I went out into the hallway and shouted for her. She wasn't far. I heard her come running. When I came back, Ernest reached for my hand and I held on to it.

"Stay, please," he said. "Don't leave before me."

I could feel his panic like static through the tips of his fingers. I'm surprised my heart didn't swell and burst free of my chest at that, his fear, his brave smile when our eyes met. I'm surprised Dawn didn't have to get down and defibrillate it, where it landed at her feet.

All at once I felt the overwhelming weight of that loss. Ernest and I could have been Father and Daughter. We might have even been friends. At the very least, we would have known each other. Hannah and Lowell stole that from us both. It was almost too much to bear.

Dawn was calm, and she knew what to do—an intravenous dose of something, a jab of something else. Ernest's face softened, and his grip on my hand did too.

"How's the pain, Ernest?" she asked.

His eyes were shut. "Magnificent."

"Still got your sense of humor, I see."

"Hanging on by a thread," Ernest told her. "Hanging on by a thread."

He pulled at my hand until I got closer and bent down to hear him speak.

"Your mother will be back soon," he whispered. "There isn't much time."

"I'm listening, Ernest," I said. "I'm here."

Nineteen

At the beginning, Ernest tried drawing Hannah, to combine his love of her with his love of art. But she was a terrible life model. She couldn't sit still. She couldn't seem to hold a thought in her head long enough for him to get it onto the canvas. He said, "It was like trying to see into a woman made of chrome."

He didn't think that he might actually be getting a clear picture of who she was becoming—all surface, all restlessness and emptiness and boredom. She'd erased her past so effectively that there was nothing left.

After a few months, she couldn't bear to be alone with him. Once they were married, Hannah filled the house with people. She said if they weren't allowed to live in London, then London would have to come to them. She never tired of flaunting her new money before her friends. Lowell Baxter was a regular fixture, apparently—dark and striking, the planes and lines of his face so accurate, so perfect that he seemed to be made of something different from the rest of them—he and Hannah both.

"Of course," Ernest told me, "that wasn't his name then. When I knew him, his name was William Lowe."

"That's who you searched for?"

"It's why I didn't find you."

Ernest couldn't stand Lowell, from the first moment. He said he oozed into the house like floodwater, coating everything in the same dark matter, cutting off its air supply. Hannah said Ernest was just jealous.

"He's harmless," my mother told him. "It's me you should be worried about."

Most mornings, while Hannah slept, Ernest went to work in a converted grain store behind the house. It was invisible, just like he was. You'd never guess it was there, if you didn't know. From the outside it's just a wind-ravaged, tumbledown outbuilding. Inside, you step down into a cube with enough glass in its ramshackle roof to flood the place with natural light.

My mother didn't set foot in there, not once. She didn't notice when he left to meet dealers in London or Paris or Amsterdam or New York. She never wondered where Ernest was when he was gone. She wasn't interested in what he was doing or when he might be coming back. She just enjoyed the time without him.

He said, "For our first anniversary I bought her a Chagall painting."

"Which one?" I asked Ernest. "Is it *The Promenade*? I think I've seen it downstairs."

Green prism hills and houses, a pastel pink church, a red crumpled picnic blanket, and a man, trapping a bird with one hand and holding on to his weightless, floating lover with the other. Ernest said it was meant to be a celebration of Chagall's blissful marriage to Bella Rosenfeld. But when he saw it, he could only think the man was anchoring her there to stop her from getting away.

My mother left Ernest seven times. Sometimes he only knew where she was because of the credit card bills—restaurants in Nice and Copenhagen, spas in Morzine and Milan, department stores in London and New York. He hardly survived the first time she left. It got a little easier each time. The second and third, he couldn't eat, or think, or breathe. But he could work. When Hannah was away, he said that was all he did.

"Dealing art?" I asked.

"I made money," he said, nodding, "and I stored it like a dam against the possibility of her leaving me for good. She always came back to the money, like an ant to sugar."

They lived like that for more than five years. And then one morning Hannah came into the kitchen and stood across from him at the table. Ernest was just getting up. She was on her way to bed. She turned to look out at the garden, and he remembered the first time she had stood there, and all the fine, groundless things he had hoped for them, at the beginning. He saw in that instant that it was he alone who had fallen in love, more with the thought of being needed and the idea of not being alone than with her.

"I'm pregnant," she said, and with a sharp laugh added, "God knows how."

Ernest put his cup down, got up and walked to where she was standing. He put his arms around her, and Hannah burst into tears.

"She cried?" I said. "Hannah cried? I've never seen her do that."

She cried while he put her to bed. She cried while he told her friends that it was now time to go home. She cried while he cooked and cleaned, while he painted and repainted the nursery. She cried because the party was over, and he wouldn't let her drink. She cried because she felt like a whale, and couldn't sleep, and had to pee every five minutes. Ernest put up with her whining and wallowing because finally it wasn't all for nothing. He put up with it for their coming child—for me, I suppose, because at last, he said, he was dealing with something that was perfectly real.

I read somewhere that Fibonacci's Golden Ratio is the mathematical principle of beauty, 1:1.62. Leonardo da Vinci called it the divine proportion, like God had a tape measure or something. A perfect face is 1.62 times longer than it is wide. A body should be 1.62 times longer from the belly button to the feet than from the same spot to the top of the head. A nose should be 1.62 times narrower, at its widest point, than a mouth. It's simple. Everything in art and architecture and nature obeys the same rule. If a thing doesn't measure up, it's not beautiful, and that isn't a matter of opinion, it is a mathematical fact. Fibonacci came up with his golden ratio, his perfect number in nature, while he was watching rabbits screwing. It is the best reason I can think of to be less judgmental about how other people spend their time.

According to Fibonacci, I'm not beautiful. No big surprise. None of my numbers are right, and that's fine by me. But according to Ernest, I was better than Da Vinci's *The Last Supper*, and Michelangelo's *The Creation of Adam*, and Botticelli's *The Birth of Venus*, and Georges Seurat's *Bathers at Asnières* and Burne-Jones's *The Golden Stairs*, all flawless examples of the divine proportion in action. Bullshit, obviously; the final ramblings of a fond and dying man, but Ernest persisted.

He said, "You were the first time I had ever, in my life, preferred real life to art."

I was born three weeks early, by Caesarean section, and I don't think my mother will ever forgive me for those scars. Afterward, she slept and Ernest stayed up, watching me in my plastic fishtank crib. There were wires attached to my chest. He said I jerked and shuddered in my sleep, as if all of my dreams were about falling, and my hands opened and closed like tiny stars. He said I was no bigger than a bird.

We were in the hospital for a week. The midwives talked only to Hannah, as if Ernest were just there to carry the bags, but he listened because he knew it would be him taking care of me.

169

"She did love you," he told me. "But the routine of it was too dull for her. I knew that something as demanding as a child would fail to pin her down for long."

It was a warm, dry summer. Ernest fed and bathed and dressed me. He read to me in the garden, and I kicked at my blankets in the shade of the old sycamore tree. He sang me to sleep, all the songs and rhymes he remembered from his own childhood. He stopped working. When I was born, Ernest lost interest in money.

He said, "Your mother found that very hard to comprehend."

For nearly three years, he took care of me while she took up her life where she'd left off. The house filled with people again, and Hannah's trips away grew longer and closer together. Ernest stayed behind. He says he was with me when I saw my first moon, my first horse, my first bird's egg, and my first puddle. Ernest was with me, not Hannah. It was him I went to if I fell and hurt my knees. It was him I looked for when I had a fever or a question or a gift.

I didn't understand. How could I have forgotten I was loved so much and by someone my mother only taught me to hate? Why would she do that to us? I felt as empty as I was angry, as bereft as bitter. Something curdled in my stomach, sour and wrong, like milk and lemon.

I wished more than anything that I could remember, and I said so. Ernest looked sadder than I'd ever seen him, and nodded.

"So do I," he said. "So do I."

The day after Hannah's thirtieth birthday, the weekend crowd had thinned and straggled home, but Lowell's car squatted low on the drive, coiled and mean-looking, like something about to pounce. Hannah came around the side of the house. She hadn't meant to bump into Ernest. He said he could tell by the look on her face.

He asked her where she was going.

"I'm leaving you," she said. "I'm not coming back."

I was in the back of Lowell's car. Ernest could see me. I was playing with my teddy bear.

"I've tried," she said, "because you're so dependable and *so* rich. And you're a good babysitter, Ernest, you always have been. But I can't do it anymore. I can't stand you."

"You can't just take our daughter," he told her. "It's illegal. I can stop you from doing that."

For a moment, Hannah looked like she almost felt sorry for him, and then the steel shutters came down behind her eyes.

"Just watch me," she said.

● ● ●

"William appeared to have some money of his own back then," Ernest told me, and I had to remind myself who he was talking about, remember that William was Lowell. "And with the money Hannah took from me, they must have thought it would last longer than it did."

Ernest said she never would have left him if she'd known that everything was on credit, all borrowed against Lowell's ambition, the power of his positive thinking and astronomical self-belief.

"How do you know all that?" I said.

"I had him investigated. William Lowe. Bankrupt, defaulted, then gone. He vanished, owing thousands. I always thought your mother would come back to me when she found that out."

"And you'd have let her?"

"I'd have done anything, Iris, to see you."

Twenty

Whenever I think about a fire, I trace it back to its very beginning, when it's still nothing, when it hasn't even happened yet. An unstruck match, an unwanted cigarette end, each humble thing on the edge of greatness, each thing giddy with potential. I think about fires in forests and cities and hillsides.

I thought about the tiny seed of hatred Hannah planted in me the first time she told me about my real father, about Ernest—the little sparks of rage she fanned when she said he didn't want me, wasn't interested, hadn't cared.

And I'd been thinking the same way about Thurston, trying to isolate the moment things started falling apart, the misplaced card that caused all the other cards to fall. I couldn't help what my mother had done, but what happened with Thurston was my fault. I'm sure of it.

Thurston made something for me. That's all he did. He asked me to meet him, and he said I should bring a candle.

"But no gas," he said. "This isn't a bonfire night."

"Well, what is it, then?"

"It's a gift," he said. "You've got to see it. It's all for you."

The address he gave me was downtown, near the church on Hill Street that looks like a club. Thurston wasn't there, but at the corner I could see the flickering lights of other candles spread out on the sidewalk, so I went that way. There were a few people there who had come out of the church mostly, I could tell from the loud slogans on their T-shirts: SO LOVED and GET YOUR BRAVE ON. I could tell from their too-good-to-be-true smiles. It was a shrine to someone. I kept walking, and when I got right up to the middle of it, I saw it was a shrine to me. Thurston had tied flowers to the railings and left notes and pictures as well as candles. I could see almost all of them were his, more than ten photos and drawings of me— different sizes, some covered with plastic, some faded and softened already by the heat of the sun and the damp, humid nights. It must have been there for a few days already. People had started to add their own best wishes and souvenirs. I watched someone leave a single rose. I saw a woman and her daughter stop to look, and frown at each other with their hands on their hearts, and move on. Somebody lit my candle, and I put it on the ground with all the others. I read a few of the messages, SUFFER LITTLE CHILDREN TO COME UNTO ME, AND FORBID THEM NOT. LIGHT A FIRE IN HEAVEN IRIS B. GONE BUT NOT FORGOTTEN xoxo. He'd drawn my eye too, right there on the ground—the sharp black pupil, the clean white ball, the swirling bright circle of color.

"Shit," I said, under my breath, and I was thinking that this pretend, dead Iris had more friends than me. I was thinking that if I really died, nobody would leave notes like that, or flowers. There would be no drawings or photos or soft toys. I was almost jealous of her. It made me more sad than anything else. It was a lousy present.

I stood up and looked around for Thurston because he'd be there somewhere on the edge of it, enjoying himself, watching the thing he'd made become more than the sum of its parts. I should have kept my head down, because that was when some- one recognized me. A girl about my age with tight, pulled-back hair and wide black eyes, dilated like hollows, pointed at me, and her mouth kind of fell open, and I suddenly knew this was what Thurston had been hoping for all along. I was the girl who showed up at her own shrine. I was Lazarus. Somebody reached out and touched me. Someone else took my picture. The news passed between them like a current, like electricity. They didn't take their eyes off me, and they talked to one another like I couldn't hear them, like I wasn't really there. "Is that her?" "Did she say something?" "Does she have a message?" "What's going on?"

One of them made the sign of the cross. Some guy dropped to his knees right there in front of me.

"It's not real," I said. "It's a joke. It's just a bad joke," and I tried to back away, but they were behind me too, stopping me, and there were more of them than before. I was stuck. I was surrounded.

I felt Thurston before I saw him. He came up behind me, flipped something over my head and walked me out of there and out of sight, super quick. They shouted at us. A few of them followed. We hid in a doorway down the block.

The hood was still over my head, and Thurston shielded me from the street, his chest pressed up against my back. I was on the very edge of something, right there in that doorway, I could see it was about to happen, but instead I just got angry, because angry was way easier to do. I rammed my elbow hard into his ribs.

"What the hell was that for?" he said, stepping back fast. It shocked him, my fury. I don't think he'd seen it before.

"Screw you," I said.

"You didn't like it?"

"No, I hated it."

"People have been paying their respects for days," he said.

"That's your gift to me?" I asked him.

He said I was the miracle those people could take home and give thanks for before dinner. "You are their proof of the existence of God."

"Are you mocking me?" I said. "Don't do that, Thurston. Don't you do that."

"Don't you get it, Iris? I thought you'd get it."

He was right. I did get it. It was classic Thurston, and I should have rolled with it and played along. But for some reason I'd decided to fight him, and even though half of me wanted to, I couldn't seem to back down.

"You think people don't see you," he said. "You think you're forgettable. But those people saw you. They won't forget."

"I don't want people to see me," I said. "Not like that."

"Sure you do. You're always saying stuff about it."

"Don't make me the butt of one of your jokes ever again," I told him. "Not without asking."

"Iris," he said. "What is this?"

177

I didn't say anything.

"Aren't we good friends?" he said. "Better than that?"

"I don't know," I told him. "I don't know what we are."

"What does that even mean?"

I shrugged.

"What do you want from me, Thurston?" I said. "Do you want me to be grateful?"

He shook his head. "How come you can't see how much you're loved?"

But I couldn't look at him. When someone puts you high up like that, in the end it's just farther to fall.

"Just leave me alone," I said.

"IRIS," Thurston said. "What are you talking about?"

I said some things to him then. I was mean.

"Who are you?" I said. "You show up, you pull stunts and play tricks and put on a show. But who are you? You've never told me one thing about yourself. I don't even know where you live. In fact, I know nothing about you."

"You know me," he said. "Come on, Iris, you do."

"You're not real," I said. "You're not honest. You're all performance. Everything is one precious fucking *moment* to you."

"What do you mean?" he asked me, and I could see all this

178

darkness in his eyes, all this doubt and vulnerability that he'd never trusted me with, never once thought to share with me. It made me so mad.

"I don't think we should see each other for a while," I said. But I didn't mean it. As soon as I'd said it, I wished I could take it back. I guess I was just trying to break something before it got broken, which is stupid. I've been paying for it ever since.

"Are you serious?" Thurston said.

"Yes, I'm serious," I lied. "Why wouldn't I be?"

"I'm SORRY," he said. "I told you I'm sorry."

"Not good enough," I said.

"If you go now," he said, "I swear to God, I'll—"

"You'll what, Thurston? You'll fucking what?"

And because I was angry with him, I walked away before he could tell me.

I shouldn't have said what I said. I should have laughed, and taken his hand and gone with him to the beach or the hills or wherever he asked me to go. But those were the last words I said to Thurston. It was the last time I saw him before we left.

That week I looked for him in all the usual places, but he wasn't there. Not by the bread shop on Monday, not in Griffith Park on Tuesday, or at my apartment building on Wednesday and

Thursday, or outside school on Friday morning with a plan, like always. He stayed away because I told him to, but really it was the last thing I wanted.

Friday afternoon in class, I was going crazy. I'd had enough. I stole a key to one of the upstairs storage closets. I walked through the halls, quiet and empty apart from my footsteps because everyone else was in class. The closet was just a room, shelved from floor to ceiling, quiet and dark and dusty, stacked with textbooks and art paper and old costumes and equipment. The door was heavy and it swung shut quick behind me and I should have checked that I could open it again but I didn't. I was in too much of a hurry. I didn't even look for the light switch. I just leaned against the wall in the dark.

The matchbook was in my pocket, tight against my hip. Flat, blue-black, glossy, it fit neatly in the palm of my hand. The matches were planted in two tight rows, one behind the other, lined up together underneath the cover, white with black tips. Lowell had left it in his coat. It had someone's phone number scrawled on it, someone's lipstick mark—not Hannah's. One match was torn off. A scar ran across the base where it had been struck. There were thirteen left.

I lit one and put it to the corners of some old posters stuck up behind me on the wall. I dropped one into a nest of old papers. I tore the pages out of some books on a shelf, crumpled them in my fists, and set them alight as well. Everything was dried out and happy to burn. The only light in the room came from the flames.

I set fires in all four corners of the room and stood in the middle watching them lick and snap and spread together. Shadows reared up against the walls. The shelves caught fire, and then the stacked tables and the frame of the door. The heat began to bend itself tightly around me, and things began to break and flare and pop. I heard the rumble in the air the fire made, like faraway thunder, like a herd of distant cattle, and then the air began to spit and hum and crackle. I tried the door handle, but it wouldn't move. I did it again, but the lock was stuck shut. I couldn't get it open. My hair started to shrink and sizzle in the heat. I could taste fire in my mouth. My eyes were scorched and dry, and my lungs were already heaving with the smoke.

Nobody heard me banging on the door, not at first. I think I was coughing, bent over on the floor in the raging dark when they broke it down. I think they smashed the lock with an axe. The fire leapt out into the hallway like a caged lion. I heard them all as if I were underwater. I saw them from behind glass. The blood moved through my veins like molasses, everything slowed down and sticky. My throat burned raw and my chest felt weighted down with concrete, wrapped in iron.

The alarm was wailing, and I realized it had been wailing for some time before it reached me. The janitor and a couple of teachers swooped in with their eyes rolling in their heads and the fire extinguishers spoiling everything with white foam. When they saw me, they started yelling and one of them dragged me out into the hallway and covered me with a coat, or a blanket. One of them stayed with me. He didn't touch me, but I could hear his voice, and he was telling me over and over that things were going to be OK. As if he knew.

By the time the fire truck and the ambulance arrived, the whole school had been evacuated. The place was bitter with damp smoke. Foam and ash mixed together like sludge. Everyone walked in it on their way out, spreading it about, like a blanket of snow fallen pure and spotless overnight until the people come out and spoil the morning, turning everything used and dirty gray.

I lay very still and pictured Thurston's shrine, the notes and photos, the drawings and flowers. I thought if I died now, if this fire killed me, then he'd think I was punishing him. Thurston would think that of me, even if it wasn't true.

"All for you," he had said, and I was shocked at myself, at the way I'd reacted, and at what I'd just almost done.

At the hospital, I had to wait for someone to come and claim me. One of the teachers who found me stayed in my room like a prison guard. Mr. Banks, from the biology department. Everything about him was the color of cement, his shirt and slacks and tank top, his shoes and hair and skin. He looked just like a statue propped there against the wall, so I pretended he was one, and ignored him.

I got a psychiatric evaluation. Actually I got three. The nurse, then the doctors, then a social worker asked me the same prying, obvious questions about my levels of happiness and any trouble at home. They asked me if I had meant to hurt myself, or hurt others. I said no to both. I said it was a stupid accident. I said I wasn't a self-harmer, nothing like that, and they looked at me like they'd heard it all before, which they probably had, but not from me.

They dressed my burns and filled me with fluids and antibiotics. They treated my scalded lungs with pure oxygen and raised their eyebrows meaningfully at each other over my head. I didn't want to speak to any of them.

They couldn't get ahold of Hannah or Lowell. Big surprise. Both of their phones were turned off. I was in no fit state to leave, they said, not until they were satisfied with my progress, and definitely not without a parent or guardian. I wanted to see Thurston then more than I'd ever wanted anything before. I wanted to say *thank you* and *sorry* and *please, please help me get the hell out of here.* But my clothes were gone. My lungs were the size of tea bags. I couldn't have escaped if I tried.

I heard them talk about hospitalizing me. They discussed hypoxia and presentation of symptoms and lack of cooperation. A fly was trying to find its way out through a window. It was drilling a hole through the glass with its wings. It wouldn't give up. There was a fly like that inside my body. I could feel it drilling in my skull.

When my mother finally arrived, she was sweating under her makeup, all the careful layers of basecoat and highlight and concealer starting to melt. I could smell the vodka on her breath from ten feet away. She was in the mood for a fight, and I worried she'd had just enough alcohol to start one and just too much to be able to win it. I picked at the bandages on my hands and kept my mouth and my eyes shut tight. I pretended none of this was happening, not to anyone I knew and definitely not to me.

She stood outside in the hallway with Mr. Banks and lied at the top of her voice. He was trying to say something sensitive and understanding, he wanted to demonstrate the school's concern, but my mother wasn't buying into it. Never own up if you can help it. That was the Baxter way. Every time he opened his mouth to speak, she cut him off.

She said, "There is no way this fire was started by my daughter."

She said the school was negligent. She said there must have been something dangerous in the storeroom for it to burst into flames like that with a child inside it.

She said, "Have you got video surveillance in that closet? No? Then good luck proving it."

She said, "You are very lucky something worse didn't happen to her on school property. You should be grateful nobody else got hurt. You should be grateful *we* are not suing *you*."

The social worker and one of the doctors took Hannah into another room down the hall. I could still hear her voice, raised high above the others. I wondered how long my mother would pay attention before she decided she needed a cigarette, or another drink, or just to get the hell out of there because everyone was so serious and ordinary and ugly and she didn't belong. She hated being made to feel like the responsible adult. They asked her if she'd brought me any fresh clothes. She looked at them like they were the ones not taking this seriously.

"I. Was. At. Lunch," she said.

I stayed in the hospital overnight. The next day, when Hannah reappeared, with just a pair of jeans, they gave me a hospital T-shirt and let me leave as an outpatient. I had strict instructions for the next twenty-four hours, a follow-up appointment to check on my burns. Hannah signed all the necessary forms and paid with a check that wouldn't cash. I saw her write down the wrong address and phone number. There wasn't any money for medical bills. We wouldn't be coming back.

It wasn't just the thing with Thurston. I'd heard them arguing about money every night for weeks before I did it. They owed nearly twenty grand in bills and back rent. Their credit cards were maxed out. Hannah was drunk and online, trying to book plane tickets back to the UK. Lowell didn't want to go.

"What choice do we have?" she hissed at him. "We came out here so you could make it, and you clearly haven't."

Lowell groaned. "It's your nut-job daughter's fault I didn't get that miniseries," he said. "Who lit a fire upstairs when the casting director was here? I had that role in the bag before she assaulted his kid."

Hannah carried on typing. "Well my nut-job daughter is going to need medical help at this rate, thousands of dollars' worth. She's a lawsuit waiting to happen. Let's get her back to the NHS, shall we? Let's get her back to her bastard millionaire father and tap him for some cash."

"She's ruined everything, your stupid kid," Lowell told her.

Hannah sloshed more vodka into their glasses. "Believe me, I've thought about that more often than you have. It's time to get out before she burns down a mall and everyone knows our business. Drink to it, Lowell. Give it up. It's time to go."

When we got outside the hospital, I looked for Thurston on the street, even though I knew he wouldn't be there. Everybody was him for half a second, until they weren't.

My mother stopped and lit a cigarette. Her hair was coming loose, and a strand of it was stuck to the hot skin of her neck. She looked up and then down Sunset Boulevard, getting her bearings, and then we set off heading west and turned right, toward Barnsdall Park. Hannah was tall as a giraffe in her Louboutins.

"That is the only time I do that for you," Hannah said. "Next time you're on your own."

"Can we take a cab?" I asked. "I feel kind of light-headed."

"No money for cabs," Hannah said. "I used my last twenty getting here." She showed me her empty wallet and pulled a sad face. "The cupboard is bare. You can rest when we get home. You can go to bed, and you can damn well stay there."

We walked down Vermont and turned left on Hollywood. I felt weak and hollow and dizzy. I thought my lungs were going to break out of my chest. In the park, I watched a little boy running wide, joyful circles around his dad. I saw a family lying back on a picnic blanket. Somebody tall and skinny walked toward us on the path, and I willed it to be Thurston, come to rescue me, but of course it wasn't, he didn't. The boy was tall and skinny, but he was a disappointment, a total stranger, and he walked right by.

"So," Hannah said, not looking at me, "I know you started that fire. The question is, did you admit it?"

A breeze moved in the leaves around us. I could see it passing. I could see where it went.

"No," I said. "But they probably know."

"For God's sake," she yelled at me. A couple of people looked over.

"What," I said, "did I ruin everything?"

"Is there anything we failed to give you?" Hannah asked. "Do you lack for anything, anything at all?" and because I didn't know how to even begin answering that question, I didn't try.

"You'll end up in a madhouse, or a prison. Arson is a very serious offense."

"They're called psychiatric hospitals," I told her. "You don't say madhouse. You don't say madhouse, and you don't say nut-job."

Hannah turned on me, jabbing her pointed finger against the flat, sore bones of my chest. "You do *not* get to tell me what I do and don't say, young lady. Not now and not ever. Is that clear?"

"You're upset about paying for it, aren't you?" I said. "If I get in trouble. If I get locked up, or institutionalized." And Hannah slapped me then, across the cheek, which I took as a yes.

She walked on ahead of me a few paces and then she said, "You've burned our bridges. That's what you've done." She stopped abruptly on the narrow path, flinging her hands toward the trees like she was asking what she'd done to deserve such hardship.

"It won't happen again," I lied. "I won't get caught again."

That last part was the truth.

Twenty-One

Ernest knew for certain he was dying three months before we came back. He said the doctor who passed on his death sentence was young and immaculately dressed and carefully sympathetic.

"Nice socks," Ernest told him after the bad news, after he'd taken it in and found that he was still breathing. The socks were pink with red spots. Ernest said you couldn't miss them.

The doctor looked lost for a second, like an actor asked to come out of character, and then he smiled and said, "Thanks. My daughter gave them to me."

Ernest felt the word *daughter* like a blade in his side. He said he'd had a daughter once but he'd lost her.

"I'm so sorry," the doctor told him. "Did she die?"

Ernest was getting ready to leave the exam room. He'd already put on his jacket.

"Honestly?" he said. "I have no idea."

All the way home he said he thought harder than ever about where I might be at that precise moment, what I might be doing, living or dead. He thought about his doctor, charged with the task of telling him that after all the chemo and radiation and surgery, there was nothing more to be done. He thought about what he might say to the next patient, and the one after that, in life-changing fifteen-minute slots, all day long, until he could go home and put his pink and red polka-dot feet up, and be with his daughter, and try to forget.

Ernest said, "I thought about everything but the facts in front of me, because I didn't want to think about those."

Even while the doctor was explaining it all, a large part of Ernest decided he was wrong. It was the only way to put one foot in front of the other, the only way he could stay upright and get through the waiting room, out into the parking lot, drive from one street to another until he reached home. I suppose his brain was hardwired to ignore the truth so it could get on, until the very last second, with the business of living.

191

But what if death is the one and only way that you do get to live forever? If the weight of the universe never changes, regardless of who's living and who's dying, that must mean we never leave it, not entirely. If I become a scrap of smoke and dust, if Ernest's ashes get flung high into the wind from his upstairs windows, if Thurston's body falls to the bottom of the sea, if Lowell's is picked apart by birds and Hannah's is buried and melts slowly back to soil, aren't we all still somewhere? Aren't we all still here?

Death might be the one true fact, the one thing you can rely on, but nobody wants to hear about it. You start trying to put a positive spin on the whole idea, and you can clear the room quicker than a bad DJ at a wedding. Death is off-limits. That's why we put a hood on the executioner. No one wants to see his face.

I told Ernest that if I could, I'd come from the planet Tralfamadore, where time is like a stretch of the Rocky Mountains, and moments are like clusters of beads on a string, laid out before you, all there at once. There is no cause and effect, no before or then or next or after. There is no difference between what was, or is, or will be. You can exist and not exist on the same string, at the same time. "You can be dead and still alive," I said, "if you're a Tralfamadorian."

Ernest laughed, and the world's oceans gathered in his chest and tried to drown him. "Who said that? When can we go?"

"It's Kurt Vonnegut," I said. "He died already. If there's such a thing as the afterlife, you'll have to look for him when you get there."

Ernest had never read any Kurt Vonnegut. I pitied him and envied him all at once, that he'd missed out and that he had it still to come. I told him that Vonnegut was a prisoner of war in Dresden and a witness to the Allied bombings in 1945. He came up from underground and almost everyone was dead, almost everything burned to the ground. He was twenty-two years old. He had a lot to make sense of, and after more than twenty years of trying not to think about it, he wrote *Slaughterhouse-Five*.

Thurston read that whole book to me out loud. He lay with his head in my lap and the book between him and the sun. It took about a week. I had never been happier.

"I'll read it to you," I told Ernest, "if we have time."

We didn't.

I tried to see Ernest's life as a string of beads. I looked at pictures of him as a young man, balancing on a fence post, leaning against a wall, squinting into the sun. I found a photo of their wedding day, he and my mother on the steps of the registry office, and below them a woman pushing a stroller, the blur of a cyclist, and a man out walking his dog.

"Why didn't you just get divorced?" I asked him.

"I needed her signature. I couldn't find her."

"But if someone disappears for that long," I said, "surely—"

"She's still my wife," he said. "My next of kin."

He looked again at the wedding picture.

"I can't still be there now," he said, "because everything is different."

Ernest was right. This isn't the planet Tralfamadore, or anything like it. Everything here is bound by beginning and end, apart from the universe, which is not only infinite but also expanding. I have a problem with something infinite getting any bigger, and I had a problem with Ernest's death. I needed a stop sign, a pause button. Not quite, not now, not yet.

Ernest said I shouldn't worry. He said he was close enough to see it quite clearly, and given that he couldn't stop it if he tried, he might as well admit, it wasn't such a long way down.

I kept it in because he didn't need to hear it. I stayed quiet because you can't make a person feel bad for dying. But the truth is, all I could think was it's a much steeper fall when you're the one left behind.

Twenty-Two

Ernest's last few days were strange and slow and fragile. We were very careful with each other. Every single thing we said and did seemed to have weight, seemed important. We were learning to live with it, I suppose, with what we knew for sure was about to happen. We were separate, like islands. He was separate, anyway. Part of him had already sailed.

Hannah stayed away, just as Ernest demanded. She had her check and seemed to have lost interest in the whole thing, happy to take the Bentley, to come and go as she pleased. I figured she left because, to her, dying is so unglamorous and wretched and contagious and she didn't want any part in it. Whatever. I was grateful for the space, the alone time, just Ernest and me, together, at the end. Lowell phoned once or twice while Hannah was still there, but only to talk about how good the catering was on set and how humble and down-to-earth the other actors were, like they were from another galaxy or something. He never called to engage with what was actually happening, in the real world, to us.

On his last whole day, we carried Ernest downstairs, the nurses and me, and laid him in the garden, with cushions and blankets and oxygen and the sun on his face. I stayed near him, building the base for a bonfire. I'd told him I would have to have one to say good-bye. He watched me while I worked, and I knew what he was doing. I went over and slipped my arm through his and said, "Stop it," but he'd already done it. It was too late. He'd been doing it for days now, picturing the world without him in it. He was erasing himself from his usual place, withdrawing, saying good-bye, because it seemed like the right thing to do.

Ernest said it was a bit like being in love with someone who doesn't love you back. The very fact that they don't need you makes them a thousand times more desirable and beautiful and the object of your devotion. Sometimes it's the impossibility of a thing that makes it irresistible. And right then, being alive was the thing he was in love with, the thing that didn't care if he was there or not. Every leaf, every blade of grass, every bug and footprint and pebble was bathed in a new kind of light for him. I knew I couldn't see it the way he could. Every single thing Ernest looked at was breathtakingly, effortlessly, perfectly itself. Even the most ordinary thing he could think of—a dustbin, a lamppost, an envelope—was part of the biggest, most persuasive, most extraordinary miracle there is, as solid as a rock and at the same time as fine and breakable as a single hair.

He said, "When you know for certain you are losing a thing, you suddenly see how much you have loved it, and how you ought to have taken better care of it all along."

It was dark when he died. Outside, bands of mist dropped onto the garden, obscuring everything, and then were just as suddenly gone. I sat with him, with Jane and Lisa and Dawn, me with my feet and my knees pressed together, my hands in my lap, my face composed, because I had no say in anything else but my own reaction. I tried to hold him with me in the room, to keep him there, but I couldn't do it. There was a storm coming and the trees thrashed in the wind. The air bellowed and cracked and the rain began to lash against his windows, louder and louder, until there was a noise above me like a filling sail, like a parachute opening. I pretended it was the sound of angels landing. I pictured a legion of them on the roof, their wings cumbersome and wide, punching great holes in the air. I thought maybe they had come for him. He was ready to go. I figured that's what happens when you get that close. It's just a step down, no big deal. I hoped so anyway. I hoped he was watching us by then from another place entirely, somewhere quiet and painless and apart. And while I was hoping, and holding his hand, he slipped away.

They left me alone with him. For a while he was still warm, and I convinced myself that he wasn't all gone, that part of him still occupied the high corners of the room. I stroked his hand, slack and heavy now, his emptied skin like a breeze on the surface of still water. I'm sure I spoke to him, but I don't remember what I said. Ernest's face was the same and not the same, a quiet house, his lips bloodless and tight as if stitched to his teeth, his flesh deflated like punctured dough, sunk and settled closer to its bones. It shocked me how quickly he abandoned it. He was there, and then suddenly and utterly, he wasn't. Dead doesn't look like sleeping. Dead looks gone.

Some of his things were on the bedside table. His watch, his toothbrush, a comb—everyday objects that seemed instantly, overwhelmingly significant because they were his, or had been, and useless too, because he would never need them again. There was a book and a half-finished crossword, and I knew already that I'd start reading it, that I'd solve the last few clues in an effort to inch nearer to him now that he was so finally and irretrievably lost. Pointless, I knew, too late, but I'd do it anyway.

Dawn came back in with her head bowed and her hands clasped. I heard her voice from very far away. I was a wasp in a jar, and she was talking to me. She told me that Ernest didn't suffer, that he wasn't in any pain.

"He knew what was coming," she said, "and he wasn't alone. You were with him, and he wasn't afraid."

I wondered if she said that to everyone. Even so, I was grateful. I wanted very much for some of it to be true.

The world doesn't end when the world ends, by the way; it keeps right on turning. The world ends, and you get up and put your clothes on and brush your teeth and eat your breakfast like nothing has changed at all. It made me sick to my stomach after Ernest died that I still found things funny, that I still got hungry or tired or bored or distracted, that after a while I started to forget about him for whole minutes and hours and days at a time. It made me want to burn something down, that I'd spent so many years acting like he didn't exist when he was right there all the time. I didn't think I could ever forgive my mother for what she did. I could have set fire to every last thing in the world she possessed, and it wouldn't have begun to change how I felt about that.

After Ernest died, when I couldn't sleep, I found myself looking for him everywhere, waiting for him to come back. I didn't find him in the drawers of mildewed papers I emptied, in the pockets of his camel-colored overcoat. He wasn't smiling from the countless drawings of faces at crowded tables, of long-ago parties and marble statues and elegant cities, all the sketches that he asked me to clear out and round up and burn. He wasn't in the half-drunk bottle of milk in the fridge. I saw it and it felt like an insult, like a punch in the stomach, that the milk was still fresh and Ernest was gone forever.

I looked at more old pictures—a freckled boy with strong cheekbones and straight teeth and an undiluted light in his eyes. I hadn't seen them before. I was sure I'd looked in that photo album and found nothing. One last check and there he was, smiling right at me from forty years ago. It felt like an extra moment of his life, an instant's grace. I figured then that as long as I could keep finding new things about him, Ernest wouldn't be completely dead. That's what I told myself anyway, so I could get up in the morning, and blink and swallow and breathe, and go through the motions of living.

Twenty-Three

The night before Ernest's funeral, I dreamed about Thurston. He was standing so close to me that I could smell the exact warm smell of his skin, even in my sleep. He didn't say a word in my dream, but when I woke up, I had the definite feeling that he'd been there, that he was nearer to me than you'd think. It faded quickly, the way dreams do, but it left traces of itself all over my morning, brief pictures of him that stopped me dead and got my heart pounding, as if he were suddenly there in the room, and I only had to turn my head to see him.

And while I pretended to myself that it wasn't impossible, while I imagined Thurston on his way, leaving home and at the airport, taking a taxi, moving toward me, something else happened. I remembered a time, back when I was little. I'd been trying and trying to find them, and suddenly there they were, these snapshots I'd been storing in my head all along.

Ernest, scooping me from my bed like feathers and carrying me outside into the cold night, into the car.

Ernest, on the driver's side, and the car rocking gently when he shut the door.

My mother's hair, loose like dark water, and the jewels on her pearly fingers glistening.

The sky's dark lavender when I sat up and the car turning down toward the sea, as if the whole world was set out below us.

I remember the tide being out, far away on the smooth gray empty sand. I've been to the beach before dawn enough times to know how it feels, like you've slipped through a seam in time, the night poised to tip over into day, but not quite, not yet. The edges of things are blurred and grainy, and you can't quite see where one ends and another begins. It's all just atoms.

I remember Ernest leaning against the car, watching the waves, Hannah stepping out of her dress and walking barefoot down the long dark stretch to the sea, her slip flowing and gathering around her like mercury in the coming light.

Him taking my hand and pulling me, squealing and leaping and gasping, across the acres of damp, sucking sand and into the cold, cold arms of the water.

Your heart stops when you go under like that, a sudden quiet in your ears and chest that fills the air like thunder as you break the surface again to breathe. I was a foundling, swimming with my clothes on. I was a water baby.

The brushed-cotton fabric of my nightdress, billowing with caught air, then clinging to my legs like a heavy second skin, trying to pull me down. Ahead, Hannah's skin flashing white against the gunmetal water as she swam.

Me and Ernest. Ernest and I. We pretended to be washed up after a shipwreck, staggering out of the water and collapsing onto the sand of a far-flung shore, coughing up deep lungfuls of ocean, clinging to life with our fingertips, until we rolled over and I let him pull me upright so we could run at the waves again.

Afterward I think we must have dragged brushwood and flotsam into a pile on the sand, parched rope and a curl-leafed book, sun-bleached branches from the straggle of trees above the dunes. Ernest showed me how to get the dry grass and the paper and twigs going, how to set them alight and how to blow on the flames to make them stronger. They pulled at me like a magnet. To stare at anything else seemed impossible, seemed plain wrong. I couldn't have looked away if I tried.

I realize now: that was my first fire, not the one in Griffith Park.

And Ernest was with me.

In the morning, I didn't think I could ever get up. I held on to those images of my father as hard as I could, when he was young and strong and I knew without question that he loved me.

Outside in the driveway, Hannah and Lowell posed like film stars. I saw Ernest's coffin in the back of the hearse and I tried not to think about him lying in there. I did my very best to look at him and smile.

"Come on, then," I said, just in case he could hear me. "Let's get this over with."

Twenty-Four

After the funeral, before my last bonfire smoldered against the darkening sky, a man introduced himself and blew open my afternoon. Tall, with gray hair, rich skin, and a charcoal-colored suit, he came up to me in the garden and smiled. I was standing with my back to the house, looking out across the fields, feeling lost.

"You must be Iris," he said.

"I am."

"You look just like Margot," he said.

"I know. Ernest told me."

He shook my hand. "I'm Alexander Brown. Did Ernest ever mention me?"

"I don't think so."

Mr. Brown smiled and said, "Good. That's very good."

"Were you friends?" I asked.

"Colleagues. For over thirty years."

"That's nice."

"I'm very sorry for your loss," he said, with his hand on my shoulder.

"Thank you. Your loss too, I guess."

He asked me to come with him. He said, "There's someone here I think you'd like to meet."

But I felt kind of rooted to the spot. I suppose I thought Ernest might still be here somewhere, watching me. What if he was right beside me and I moved away? He said he wouldn't leave the house if he could help it. I didn't want him to feel abandoned. Nobody should have to feel that.

"What? Right now?"

"I think you'll want to. I don't think you'll want to wait."

Alexander Brown slipped a scrap of paper into my hand, and when I looked down, it was there in my palm: a drawing of an eye, the round black pupil, the white outline, the bright swirl of color.

I tried to speak. I tried to say his name, but I couldn't get the air out of my chest.

Alexander Brown smiled. "He's inside the house."

"Are you kidding me?" I said, and I heard my own voice rising.

"I need you to slow down and stay calm," he said, with his hand over mine. "It's important that we don't attract attention at this stage."

"What stage?" I asked.

He didn't answer me.

I sat down hard on a window ledge. I looked up. Birds lined the rooftop of Ernest's house, looking down. They flew up like thrown papers at the first hint of something amiss, at the pop of a champagne cork, at the lick of a lit flame.

"Breathe," Alexander Brown told me, and I did. I sat there and copied his breathing, because I'd forgotten how to do it right on my own.

"How did he get here?" I said. "How did he find me?"

"Your father arranged it."

I smiled. My face broke open and light poured out. That's how it felt.

"Ernest did this? But . . ."

"Of course he did."

"But how did he find him? I searched everywhere."

208

"Your father sent the same people who never managed to find you. He made an offer."

"What kind of offer?"

"One favor for another. Would you like to see him? Have you calmed down? Shall we go?"

I looked out across the garden, at Hannah and Lowell lording their power and status over the guests. There was a cloud over the sun, soft gray and edged with brilliant light. I followed Alexander Brown into the relative dark of the house, where my best friend was waiting.

"He has something for you," he said.

"What is it?"

"Something life-changing. Eye-opening. From Ernest."

"Wait. They spoke?"

"Yes."

"Ernest talked to him?"

Alexander blinked very slowly. He said, "It is vital that you compose yourself, Iris."

I nodded and followed him through the reception rooms and into the back kitchen.

"You'll need to focus," he said.

I didn't answer him. I couldn't.

Across the room, on the other side of a river of waitstaff and canapés and empty bottles, was Thurston.

Tall, dark, skinny, pale, with his arms out ready to catch me, and smiling.

I waded in.

Twenty-Five

We found a place to be, just him and me. We walked out of the house and away from the funeral party.

"I can't believe he found you," I told him, and Thurston said, "I think that man would have done anything for you."

"So many times," I said, "I thought about how you two would have liked each other, and wished that you could have heard his voice."

"And I did," he said.

"What did he talk to you about?"

We arrived at the place in the woods I'd swept clean the night of my fire. Thurston stopped walking.

"You, Iris," he said. "He talked about you."

"And what did he say?"

Thurston reached into the inside pocket of his coat and pulled out a phone.

I laughed. "Since when do you have one of those?"

"It's not mine," he said. "It's yours. There's something on it for you."

We sat down together on the ground soft with dead leaves and pine and rich soil. When I played the message, Ernest's voice filled the air around us, drifting up toward the trees. So much better than a letter, and so strange too, his real voice after he was gone. I had to stop and start it again at the overwhelming sound of him.

"My dear Iris," Ernest began, "I am gone now, and you, I hope, are not alone. Please forgive me for speaking to you this way, a sort of confession. You have been more than patient, and I will try to explain it all, from the very beginning. From Margot."

It crumpled me, that voice. Thurston held on to my hand and we listened.

It was because of Margot that Ernest came into his line of work. She was broke and struggling, cut off without a penny, and he would have done anything to help her.

"Just as I would have done for you, Iris."

I smiled. I hung on his every word. It was a gift, I suppose, hearing him like that when he was already gone.

"Now, when I was a child, if I promised not to touch, I was allowed to stand on a chair with my face inches from the canvas and study the precise brushstrokes of Géricault's *Portrait of a Kleptomaniac* or those frantic sweeps of Van Gogh's *A Wind-Beaten Tree*. In the library overlooking our garden, my mother gave me books too heavy to carry, full of paintings and sketches. I learned how the early masters used mirrors and crystals and candles to trap an image right there on the page. How I loved studying the way the artist captured a hand or a foot or an eye."

So Ernest painted something. For Margot.

The inspiration hung in his mother's dressing room. He imagined the real subject in front of him. He measured the dimensions, and he got the whites just right. He used old paints. He'd unearthed a box of them in a cabinet somewhere, maybe from his grandfather's time. He knew enough even then to know that old materials are the lifeblood of a good forger.

"You see, my talent for mimicry went beyond just doing impressions."

Oil on canvas board, eight inches by sixteen, a Charles Courtney

Curran painting of the Grand Palais des Beaux-Arts in Paris, 1900. Ernest's first fake. He wondered what likeness he got, if any, so many hundreds of years later, in his version of a version of it.

He took it to Margot in London, took the train on his own. Margot loved it. She thought it was the original, stolen from home.

Ernest told her to sell it.

And then she phoned him, three weeks later.

"I thought you'd like to know, little brother. That little Curran you stole fetched over ten thousand pounds at auction. Look out for the postman. I'm sending you your cut."

"I didn't steal it," Ernest said. "I painted it."

Margot went quiet. She never went quiet. Then she let out a breath, and he could hear the grin in her voice before she spoke. "You little genius."

"You don't mind?"

Margot laughed. "Mind?" she said. "God, no. I'd never be such a snob. Art's art and all that. Even Michelangelo started out as a forger."

"Did they teach you that in school, Iris?" Ernest's voice asked me. "Perhaps not. When Michelangelo was a struggling artist, he tried to pass off one of his own marble sculptures as an ancient Roman statue, so he could get a better price. With the help of a dealer, he damaged and buried it, so someone would 'discover' it and trick the market. So you see, even the most famous artist in the Western World has stooped as low as me."

And Margot wanted to do it again.

Ernest wasn't sure they should, but Margot said if it was good enough for Michelangelo, it really should be good enough for them.

She found a willing art historian, a dealer and an expert in his field, and persuaded him to work with Ernest. Apparently, those are the people with power in the art market—the experts and dealers. With one dip of the head or tilt of the chin, they can make or break a fake painting. Margot met him at a cocktail party. The expert's name was Alexander Brown.

"You will have just met him, Iris, at my funeral. He will have reunited you with your friend."

I smiled at this, and Thurston squeezed my hand.

It turned out, Ernest said, that Mr. Brown was a very useful friend to have. Margot introduced the two of them.

"'If you want this opportunity,' she told me, 'you'd better seize it.'

"So I did what Margot would have done, Iris. Remember? I looked down. I jumped in."

The trick, according to Ernest, wasn't to copy a famous painter, but to become him, the way a method actor inhabits his role. He never copied existing paintings stroke for stroke—not to sell. Not after that first one. Instead, he invented other versions of them—abandoned attempts, lost prints, early sketches. He imagined gaps between works.

"Why are there forty-four documented Dalí works for the year 1932 and only twenty-eight for 1931? What did Magritte paint in 1961, after *The Memoirs of a Saint* in 1960 and before *The Great Table* in 1962?"

I didn't know, but Ernest was quick to continue.

"Art documents itself, Iris, and all a good forger has to look out for is the space between things, the blank days in the diary where you can slip in a print, a lithograph, or an undiscovered early work.

"And all of them sold," Ernest's voice said. "So judge me if you will, Iris. I deserve it. It's dishonest. I'm dishonest. I should have told you myself, but I'm afraid I couldn't. I had to take this secret with me. I hope you'll understand why."

In the beginning, he did pencil drawings in the style of Augustus John and Piranesi and Poussin. Alexander Brown sent him pieces of rare antique paper, and Ernest copied onto them, working from catalogs, not originals. But later, he sat in galleries for hours, visiting and revisiting the same works over a period of time, until he understood how they were painted, until he thought he knew just what the artist had seen and felt. The canvases hypnotized him into seeing where they started and how they were begun.

But there were some artists he could never copy, however many times Alexander Brown asked, however much money he might offer for one.

"Rothko. You can't fake a Rothko, and you're right, Iris, you can't fake an Yves Klein. You'd think they'd be easy, but they've got the artist all over them. They're the hardest of all."

He concentrated as much as anything on how a painting or drawing could make him feel. He memorized the first word that came into his head when he looked at the original, so that he could communicate the exact same thing in his efforts. Technical accuracy and trails of documents were one thing. That split second, that decisive blink of an eye, was another.

Ernest met Alexander Brown only once, with Margot. But they worked together for more than thirty years. Alexander faked records and documents to match most of the forged paintings, and allowed unsuspecting researchers and academics to find them and declare them genuine.

"A dishonest man too, Iris, a lover of money, but not a bad man in the end. I promise you that."

Together, they put hundreds of forgeries on the walls of international galleries and private collectors. They exploited the art world's obsession with authenticity to their advantage. Ernest's forgeries sold for six- and seven-figure sums, money he spent on buying genuine paintings—things his mother would have loved, investments. The money he earned by cheating he plowed straight back in. It made him feel less guilty, less like a thief.

My father's fakes were bragged about and shown off and kept under special conditions befitting priceless works by world-famous artists. But to this day, nobody has ever heard of Ernest Toby Jones because he never once got caught.

"And you know what they say about forgeries," Ernest's voice said. "The good ones are still hanging on the walls."

Twenty-Six

At the end of the message, Ernest's voice grew ragged with exhaustion.

"I can't say good-bye," he said. "Not like this. Stay with Thurston. He and Alexander will show you what happens next."

I didn't want to move. My head was spinning with everything I thought I knew and didn't know about Ernest. I didn't know how to feel, what to do with any of it.

Thurston and I sat back to back, looking up at the tops of trees, dark against the sky.

He didn't pressure me to speak. He knew I wasn't ready. After a while, he looked at his watch. "Come on," he said. "We have to get back."

"What for?"

He smiled and stood up. "Ernest saved the best for last."

"What do you mean?"

"You'll see."

There was no point asking him what was going on. The day had blown out of my hands like so much ash, like so much powdered paint, and all I could do was wait and see where it landed.

Thurston pulled me to my feet. We walked straight out of the woods and along the empty road, on a narrow strip of grass.

"So there's one more thing, something else you need to know. About a letter."

"What letter?" I asked.

"A letter that was sent here, and opened and read."

"How do you know?"

"Ernest told me," he said. "Mr. Brown will tell you the rest. Just wait."

Back at the house, Alexander Brown was talking to Hannah on the lawn. At Thurston's signal, he came inside to meet us.

"Forgive me if this is abrupt," he said. "We don't have much time. Iris, did your father ever say anything to you about a painting called *Fire Color One*?"

"He mentioned he wanted to tell me something about it. We ran out of time, though."

Alexander Brown smiled. "It's a new acquisition. And it's yours."

"Wait," I said. "Ernest owned *Fire Color One*?"

Thurston smiled too. "He chose it especially for you."

"Your friend Thurston here manned the telephone at Christie's for Ernest the week before he died."

"You did?" I said, and Thurston nodded.

"He flew me to New York before he flew me here."

Alexander Brown said, "That was the favor I mentioned. Thurston did well. He placed the winning bid. Do you want to know for how much?"

"Not really," I said. "I don't think I do."

"In excess of forty million dollars, Iris," he said. "Ernest's entire worth."

"Forty million dollars?"

"It's all yours."

I felt sick. The earth had tilted wildly on its axis, and nobody seemed to notice it but me. That was Forbes List, unforgivable, impossible rich, just like Thurston and I had always talked about. I think I reached for his hand. I think without it I would have fainted.

"Can I just keep it?" I said. "The painting, I mean?"

"You can do whatever you want with it," Mr. Brown said. "It belongs to you."

"But it doesn't make sense," I told them. "Why the hell would Hannah want me to have it? She told Ernest to let me have the new one. I heard her. Why would she say that if it was worth so much money?"

"Because of this."

Alexander handed me a piece of paper.

"Read it out loud," he said. "I like the tone of it. Read it to me."

"*We are very sorry to inform you,*" I read, "*that in light of new documentation . . . the authenticity of the work entitled FIRE COLOR ONE . . . can no longer be confirmed. If you have any concerns or queries . . . please do not hesitate to contact us. Yours . . .*"

"It's a fake?" I said. "But you can't fake an Yves Klein. Everyone knows it can't be done."

I waited for him and Thurston to stop smiling.

"You can't fake an Yves Klein," Alexander Brown said. "You're right. They're too notorious, too well documented." He paused. "But you can fake a letter. Or I can, anyway."

"So . . ." I said.

"So Hannah intercepted that letter and gave her blessing to

your inheritance," he said. "In fact, I believe it was her suggestion?"

Thurston said I wasn't supposed to see it. He said it came through the door, as planned, while Hannah was still here. It was addressed to Ernest, from Christie's in New York, and it was marked URGENT. She took it and read it, and after that, she tore it into tiny pieces and burned it.

"I remember that," I said, that sweet-sharp smell of paper, just burned, on the stairs, and her asking me if I'd done it.

Thurston nodded. "Ernest gave your mother exactly what she asked for. She has no one to blame but herself."

I looked for where she was standing out in the garden, a cluster of people around her, a good tall drink in her hand. She held herself like a coiled spring, triumph leaking through the gaps in her attempt at a somber surface.

"Then we both win," I said.

"Not quite," said Thurston.

"Let's get them in," Alexander Brown said, and I had no idea what he meant.

"What's happening?"

"A moment," Thurston said. "The best one Ernest could think of."

"Where? Here? Now?"

He nodded. "Alexander has persuaded your mother that everyone should have a tour of the paintings, before they're taken down and sold."

Before I could say anything, he put a heavy flashlight in my hand and said, "There's going to be a cut to the power. It's going to get very dark in those rooms with the curtains drawn. You'll need this."

The guests were already coming in. The room was filling up. Alexander Brown stayed with me and Thurston slipped behind a pillar as Hannah pushed her way through to the front.

"This," she said, spreading her arms wide, "is the Italian room."

The paintings weren't going to be staying here for long. When Ernest died, before he was even cold, my mother arranged for a crew from London to come after the funeral and pack them up, wrap each canvas carefully and separately in crates for collection. She made appointments with auction houses and private dealers. She was all business and forward motion. She did all that before she even asked me if I was OK. She was looking forward to record-breaking sales, to a bidding war. She was counting her chickens again. She and Lowell must have thought of nothing else.

As she stood there, in the Italian room, talking about the paintings, counting on her fingers the famous names that graced the walls, you could see it written all over her face: *hers now.* This was all hers.

Alexander Brown shifted a little beside me. He cleared his throat.

"I don't get it," I said.

"Get what?"

"How could he have spent his entire fortune on one painting?" I asked him. "How could he have paid all that money for it, with all these priceless canvases still on the walls?"

He said it very quietly, so that nobody else would hear. "What was it Ernest said—something about 'the good ones,' as he called them?"

We locked eyes for just a second, as the lights went out, and the place went black.

"Oh God," Hannah said. "What's happened?"

Alexander Brown whispered, "The Vermeer in Ernest's bedroom. The Mirós and Picassos and Modiglianis. The Renoir and the Degas and the Van Gogh and the little Gauguins. They're all fakes," he said. "Copies of the real things painted by Ernest in the years since you went missing."

It took my father twelve years to copy his collection. He sold the real works to private collectors on the contractual understanding that they didn't exhibit until a year after his death.

He played the long con.

They were brilliant forgeries. They looked the same on the surface, to the naked eye. They might even have fooled the experts, but underneath they were all worthless.

I couldn't breathe.

Hannah was still panicking about the loss of power.

"Does anyone have a light or something?" she asked.

"Iris does," Thurston said from somewhere at the back of the room, and the crowd parted to let me make my way to the front.

Hannah snatched it out of my hand and switched it on—an unexpected warm blue light that made our teeth and the whites of our eyes glow like bulbs.

"What is this, Iris?" she said, and she shone it at the wall.

Ernest had laid traps and my mother stumbled right into them. There was something beneath the surface of every painting, written in zinc white, so it would show up under ultraviolet light and stop my mother and Lowell dead in their tracks. Their world was about to end, and Ernest had made sure they had an audience. Better than a fire, better than any revenge I could

226

have ever thought of, more than twelve years in the making—a message from Ernest for them and one for me too.

Hannah shone the flashlight on each of the canvases in the room, her spare hand pressed to her mouth trying to keep in the gathering sound, her eyes like glass marbles. She ran through the hall and to the dining room and kitchen, upstairs to the bedrooms and the landing. Lowell trailed after her and some of their guests followed, the crowd dwindling, though, turning away appalled and embarrassed, until it was just my mother, alone, face-to-face with what Ernest had done.

I didn't stay to see them all. Somehow I got outside and made my way over to the stack of crates and broken furniture Hannah and Lowell had already begun to discard. I don't remember where Thurston was. I was dazed and reeling and definitely alone. I could hear my mother moving through the house, track her hysterical wailing, catastrophic, apocalyptic, and I watched as she burst through the door and onto the lawn below me.

I could hardly believe it. Ernest. My own flesh and blood, who wasn't allowed to be my father and who still, in the end, had loved me anyway, had found a way to show me just how much.

He'd painted the same word on each of the forty-seven canvases that filled the house. Bigger and bigger each time until it took up the whole space, waiting patiently, screaming out beneath layers of paint. A reminder. An affirmation. A promise.

IRIS.

In the end, I paid tribute the only way I could. With a promise of my own.

I struck a match.

And I hoped that somewhere, Ernest was watching.

Acknowledgments

Thanks Thanks Thanks to Veronique Baxter and Bob Ricard, Rachel Denwood and Liza Kaplan, and my beloved Alex, Molly, and Ella.